ARE FOREVER

Ceci Jenkinson is the author of *The Mum Shop*, the first story in Oli and Skipjack's Tales of Trouble series. *Gnomes Are Forever* is her second children's book. She lives in Wales with her husband and two young sons.

Praise for *The Mum Shop*:

'It's fresh and very funny and the Mum Shop itself is a wonderful central idea that will appeal to all ages . . . The writing zips everything nice and sharply and I shall look forward to reading more of Oli and Skipjack's adventures. I wish Ceci all the best for a sparkling future.'

Jeremy Strong, author of *The Hundred-Mile-an-Hour Dog*

Read more of Oli and Skipjack's
Tales of Trouble

The Mum Shop

Gnomes ARE FOREVER

CECI JENKINSON

ff

faber and faber

First published in 2009
by Faber and Faber Limited
3 Queen Square London WC1N 3AU

Typeset by Faber and Faber Limited
Printed in England by CPI Bookmarque, Croydon, CR0 4TD

A CIP record for this book
is available from the British Library

ISBN 978-0-571-24073-9

2 4 6 8 10 9 7 5 3 1

For J,
only without the onion pie

CONTENTS

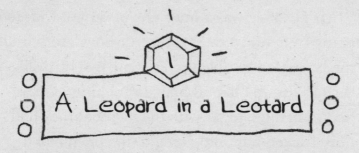

A Leopard in a Leotard

'You go first.'

'No, you go first.'

'That's not fair. I went first last time.'

'Last time doesn't count, 'cos it wasn't Mr Grimble.'

It was Saturday morning in early January at the swimming-pool bus stop, where Oli Biggles and his best friend Skipjack Haynes were waiting for the Number 11. It was raining the determined sort of rain that would have caused Noah to wring out his beard, squint up at the heavens and murmur, 'Hmm. Better build an ark.' Most of the huddle at the bus stop looked forward to stepping out of the cold, wet rain on to a warm, dry bus. But not Oli and Skipjack. This was because at the wheel of the warm, dry bus would probably be the hairy, scary

Mr Albert Grimble.

Mr Grimble was a huge ape of a man with too many teeth and a deep dislike of boys. And of all the boys Mr Grimble disliked, the two he disliked the most were Oli and Skipjack. This may have had something to do with the fact that they had once tricked him into going to the town hall to collect, from the mayor, a prize for winning a King Kong Look-alike Competition. Of course, there had been no King Kong Look-alike Competition and therefore there was no prize. But by the time Mr Grimble discovered this he was being led away from the town hall by a pair of large security guards, leaving the mayor convinced that he was completely potty.

'Here comes the bus,' said Skipjack, peering through the rain at the big red shape trundling towards them. 'And, yes – it's Gruesome Grimble.'

'I'm not getting on first,' said Oli firmly.

'Tell you what: we'll toss,' offered his friend. 'Heads you go first, tails I go second.'

Oli rolled his eyes. 'Skipjack, that only works on Slugger Stubbins, remember?' Slugger

Stubbins was the school thug and steam-roller of the Under 11 rugby team, a boy as thick as a brick.

'All right, let's get on together,' said Skipjack. 'Of course, he might not let us on at all. We must be very polite. Don't mention gorillas.'

So the boys stepped on to the bus together and chorused, 'Pond Lane, please, Mr Grimble.'

Their enemy glanced up sharply and his face darkened like storm clouds over Mount Doom.

He scowled at the boys from under a long black hedge of eyebrows. 'You two,' he growled. 'Double trouble. You've got a nerve, getting on my bus. I've a good mind to throw you off and make you walk home in the rain.'

Skipjack opened his big, brown eyes as wide as they could go.

'Oh, please, Mr Grimble. Let us on. We promise not to cause any trouble.'

'We'll be angels,' added Oli sweetly.

'Demons more like,' muttered Mr Grimble, but he printed out two tickets. As he was handing these to the boys, they noticed that his left forearm was encased in a thick white bandage.

'What did you do to your arm, Mr Grimble?' asked Oli.

'Strained it,' grunted the bus driver. 'Potatoes.'

'Dangerous things, potatoes,' Skipjack commented darkly. 'What were you doing, Mr Grimble − trying to force them into a hot oven? Or skinning them alive with a peeler?'

Mr Grimble frowned. 'If you must know, I was digging a trench to plant them in. Now, get along. I haven't got all day.'

As they moved away Oli whispered, 'It wasn't very polite of you to accuse him of torturing potatoes like that, Skip. For a moment I thought he wouldn't let us on.'

'Relax, Oli,' replied Skipjack airily. 'I think Mr Grimble quite likes us, secretly. He just doesn't want to show it.'

As he spoke the bus was filled with the piercing whine of a loudspeaker being switched on and Mr Grimble's voice came booming over the airwaves.

'Attention everybody. It is my duty as your driver to warn all passengers that two extremely naughty boys have just come on board. Watch them carefully, ladies and gentlemen, and don't let them get up to any mischief. Thank you.'

By the time Oli and Skipjack had found a pair of empty seats, every pair of eyes on the crowded bus had fixed them with a disapproving stare and the air was thick with tutting sounds and murmurs of 'That's them.'

'Quite likes us, eh?' whispered Oli, blushing furiously as he shrank into a corner seat right at the back.

'He's hiding it well,' agreed Skipjack, flopping down next to him.

In fact, the passengers' interest in the boys melted away faster than a snowflake on a nose. And why? Because on this particular morning everyone was talking about something much more exciting: diamonds. Not just any old diamonds, either: disappearing ones. A jewel thief was at work in town, and last night he had struck again. The scene of his latest crime had been Spiffing Castle, home of the tall, thin Lord and Lady Spiffing and their pack of tall, thin dogs.

A newspaper had been left on Oli's seat. He picked it up and they looked at the headline:

CAT-BURGLAR POUNCES AGAIN! DIAMOND EAR-RINGS STOLEN – POLICE BAFFLED!

'Why would he steal ear-rings if he's a cat-burglar?' Skipjack wanted to know.

'Cat-burglars don't burgle cats, Skip. They climb up the outside of buildings, like Spider-Man.'

'Well, why aren't they called spider-burglars, then?'

'I dunno. Let's read.'

Local police were left scratching their heads yesterday after a daring robbery at Spiffing Castle. 'We don't know how he got in,' admitted Sergeant Flower, 'and we don't know how he got out again. And we don't know how he found the ear-rings.'

Lady Spiffing shrugged off the loss of her precious jewels. 'They were terribly ugly,' she said. 'And after all, they were only stones and metal.'

However, Lord Spiffing was more defiant. 'If he tries to come back for my great-grandfather's diamond tie pin I shall be ready for the cheeky blighter with my Viking battle-axe.'

An old couple sitting near the boys were discussing the robbery. 'How did he get past all their dogs, that's what I want to know,' said the man.

'Well, he nearly didn't get past,' replied his companion. 'I heard that one of the dogs bit him on the arm as he was making his getaway. The left arm it was, just below the elbow.'

Oli and Skipjack exchanged glances.

'He can't be local, whoever he is,' continued the woman, 'or he would never have gone to all the trouble of climbing up the house. Everyone knows the Spiffings keep the key under the flowerpot by the back door. Come on, here's our stop.'

'The left arm,' repeated Oli, 'Just below the elbow. Potatoes, ha-ha. Skipjack my friend, I believe we have just discovered the whoabouts of the cat-burglar.'

Skipjack nodded thoughtfully. There was a gleam in his eye which his friend recognised. Oli grinned. 'Well?' he asked. 'What's the plan?'

'We must warn everyone,' said Skipjack slowly. 'It's our duty as passengers. I know – we'll make a poster.' He fished in his pocket and pulled out a crumpled swimming-pool timetable. 'Got a pencil?' he asked as he laid the paper face down on his knee and smoothed it out. Oli found a chewed stub and passed it to Skipjack, who twiddled it thoughtfully in his fingers while he frowned into space.

'We should start with "WANTED",' Oli told him. 'That's how all bad-guy posters start.'

So Skipjack wrote 'WANTED', which seemed to unlock their store of ideas and soon the poster was finished.

'We need something to stick it on the window with,' said Oli.

After a mining expedition in his pockets Skipjack extracted a grubby blue blob of sticky tack. Oli pressed their poster on to the back window of the bus and they sat back to admire it.

WANTED!
DEAD OR really DEAD
MISTER GRimble
He is a dangerous Jool
Theef leading a dubble life
By day he is a harmless
driver of the N° 11 BUS but
by nite he becomes:
CAT MAN
The lepperd in the Leotard
Help us Stop Mister Grimble
befor he strikes again!

'Perfect,' said Oli.

At the Pond Lane stop they jumped off, avoiding Mr Grimble's eye, and chuckled as they watched the bus trundle away with their poster in the back window.

'I wonder how long it'll takc him to find it,' said Skipjack.

'Ages, I hope, so loads of people have a chance to see it,' grinned Oli.

The two boys lived about five minutes' walk away from each other, so they parted at Oli's gate.

'See you tomorrow,' called Skipjack and he ran all the way home because he realised it was time for food.

After supper that evening, Oli went upstairs to write down the name of a girl he quite liked at school. He had to write it in code, in case his younger sister Tara found it. Tara was a human bloodhound; if you had a secret diary or an embarrassing list, she would sniff it out. Oli had been lumbered with two sisters, which he thought was very unfair. His older sister, Becky, lived on a teenaged dream-cloud and was not remotely interested in Oli or his secrets. Tara was the one to watch out for, so Oli and Skipjack had invented a code so complicated that it would have boggled the mind of the world's brainiest cryptologist. In fact, it often boggled the minds of Oli and Skipjack as well and it took ages to work out, which meant that they favoured girls with short names. Oli was just struggling with the final letter of this one when there was a knock at the front door.

It wasn't just any old knock – it was like the thundering hammer of a horde of bloodthirsty raiders with a battering ram. There could only be one person in the town angry enough to bash on the Biggles door like that; Oli's heart lurched and he put his ears on standby.

Sure enough, the next thing he heard was the Grimble Boom.

'WHERE IS HE?'

It was a short hop from Oli's desk to the inside of his cupboard. He could not hear the rest of the conversation from his hiding place among the shoes and cardboard boxes but he preferred it that way; he knew when it was Mr Grimble's go because his bedroom shook, and he guessed that during the quiet intervals his mum was speaking. After a while the shaking stopped and he heard his mum come up the stairs and into his room.

'Oli, come out, please.'

Oli tumbled out of his cupboard in a little avalanche of trainers and old toys.

Mum had her serious face on. 'Oli, you and Skipjack really must stop annoying Mr Grimble like this.'

'I know, but he was being really mean. He told all the passengers we were naughty.'

'You still can't put posters up on the poor man's bus saying he's a cat-burglar.'

Oli thought he heard a giggle trying to escape from his mum and he stole a glance at her. She was frowning hard, but the corners of her mouth were twitching.

'I've had to agree to a punishment,' she told him. 'Just to shut him up. I've said that you and Skipjack will go and help him dig his potato patch tomorrow morning. He's done something to his arm and he can't dig.'

'But, Mum, it's Sunday rugby tomorrow morning!'

'No buts. It was the only way I could stop the ridiculous man from going to the police. You'll just have to get there early and try to finish in time. I'll go and ring Skipjack's mum now.'

As Oli settled down to sleep later that evening, he thought about all the people on the bus who would have seen their poster and pictured Mr Grimble in a leotard. He smiled. It had been worth it.

2
Gnomes & Neighbours

'But how did he know it was us?' asked Skipjack the next morning. The boys were in Oli's mum's car, on their way to their potato punishment. Yesterday's rain had blown away in the night and it was one of those white winter mornings when the air seems to be made of invisible razor blades.

Oli shrugged. 'Just a lucky guess, I reckon. Wow, he was angry last night, Skip. He was at his most King Kong-like ever. I dunno how Mum held him off.'

'I hate people who shout,' said his mum. 'I gave him one of my Cold Looks.'

The boys gasped. 'It's a wonder he didn't turn to Ice Man,' said Oli.

'I feel like Ice Man now,' said Skipjack, jiggling up and down to keep warm. 'Boo-hoo, we're there. I hope the Grimbles' garden has central heating.'

'Give me a ring when you want collecting. Here's my mobile – and don't lose it!' called Mum as they slammed the doors.

The Grimbles lived in a small, neat house just like all the others in the same road except for one thing.

The garden was full of gnomes.

The boys looked around in astonishment. The small, brightly painted statues were everywhere. There were gnomes on toadstools, gnomes under

toadstools, gnomes with fishing rods, gnomes
without fishing rods, smiley gnomes, grumpy
gnomes, big gnomes and little gnomes. Gnomes
were peeking out from under bushes, snoozing in
the grass and chatting in cosy corners of the
patio. There was even a gnome standing at a tree
trunk with his trousers down.

'Look!' exclaimed Skipjack with delight. 'That
one's having a pee!'

Oli's attention, however, had been grabbed by
something else even more surprising. Parked in
the driveway of the next-door house was the

most beautiful car he had ever seen – a 1930s-
style red Morgan 4/4. As Oli gazed on its
gleaming paint and dazzling chrome he tried to
imagine himself driving such a beauty – it would
be awesome.

But Mr Grimble was bearing down on them,
slapping his gloved hands together and breathing
smoke through his beard. 'You're here at last,' he
grunted. 'Follow me.'

He led them to the back garden, where he
pointed a fat finger at a patch of weedy ground.
Two massive spades leant against the nearby
fence.

'That's where I want you to dig my potato
trench,' he told them. 'Two foot deep and six
foot long. A good bit of honest work will knock
you two into shape. I'm off to collect the wife
from choir practice. Well, go on – get digging.'

'This isn't honest work – it's slave labour,'
grumbled Oli as soon as they were alone.

He picked up the nearest spade with a groan.
'No wonder Mr Grimble's arms are so long –
come and feel this weight.'

If His Roman Godliness Pluto had wanted to

dig a short-cut to the underworld, Mr Grimble's spades would have been just the tools for the job. They were so big and heavy that even by ramming them at the iron-hard winter earth and jumping on them, the boys could only turn up tiny morsels of frozen soil. After ten minutes of hopping on and off his spade and scraping at the ground Oli stopped and looked with disgust at the result of his efforts.

'It's not even the beginning of a hole. It's just a scratch.'

'Mine's the same,' sighed Skipjack. 'We're going to be here all day. So much for rugby.'

Just then a cheerful whistle pierced their gloom and a

man appeared at the fence. He looked about twenty-five, with bright blue eyes and sandy-coloured hair.

''Ello, lads!' he said with a grin. 'I'm Reggie Smith, the neighbour.' He waved an empty pie tin. 'I wanted to return this to Mrs G., but I suppose she's at choir practice. That digging looks like hard work – are you doing it for love, or money?'

'Neither. We're Mr Grimble's new slaves,' grumbled Skipjack, jabbing at the ground crossly. 'We've got to make a trench for his potatoes.'

Reggie shook his head in sympathy. Then he

said, 'I think I can help. Hold on,' and he disappeared. Oli and Skipjack stopped scraping and waited. After a moment Reggie was back, wearing a thick jacket and gloves. He vaulted the fence into the Grimbles' garden and held out a small, sharp spade and a matching fork.

The boys' eyes lit up. 'Great! These will be much easier.'

'Good,' declared Reggie cheerfully. 'Now, if I get stuck in too while they're gone, we'll get a lovely trench dug in record time.'

'But, why would you want to help us?' asked Oli.

'Let's just say I've got a heart of gold.' Reggie grinned. 'Besides, I could do with some exercise.' He checked his watch. 'We've got about fifteen minutes. Mr G. always stays for a cup of tea when he goes to collect Mrs G. from choir practice.'

He picked up one of the huge spades with ease and started digging. 'What are your names, slaves?' he asked.

'I'm Oli,' said Oli, 'and this is Skipjack.'

The new tools were much easier to use, light

and sharp-edged. With Reggie helping they began to make fast headway.

'Wow, I'm hot,' gasped Skipjack after a spurt of energetic digging. 'I might even have to take my hot-water bottle off.'

While they dug the boys told their new friend the story of the poster on the bus and Reggie roared with laughter.

'Mr G. a cat-burglar,' he chuckled. 'That'll be the day.'

'Maybe he's a gnome thief,' suggested Oli, thinking of all the little statues dotted about the garden.

'The Grimbles love their gnomes,' Reggie told them. 'Mrs G. says they come alive at night and work in the garden.'

'That's slave labour,' protested Skipjack. 'Like us.'

'I gave her the gnome with the swag bag,' Reggie went on, 'to thank her for being such a lovely neighbour. She makes me onion pies.'

Oli shuddered. 'That's lovely?'

'Double lovely. Look, lads, we've nearly finished.'

'We'll be in time for rugby after all,' said Oli. 'You must be really fit, Reggie, to be such a fast digger.'

'Well, being a window cleaner, I have to run up and down a lot of ladders,' said Reggie. 'Oops, that's the Grimbles. I'd better be off.'

'Thanks, Reggie,' chorused the boys.

'My pleasure, lads. Catch you later.' Reggie hopped back over to his side of the fence and disappeared indoors.

The boys made sure they were looking very busy when Mr Grimble arrived to inspect their work. Behind him pattered a thin, beige woman with startled eyes who looked exactly like a spindly marsh bird.

Mr Grimble strode up and cast a critical eye over the trench.

'Not bad,' he muttered, 'but I wanted it wider.'

His wife peered anxiously into the pit as if a tomb-load of undead might reach out and clutch her.

'I think it's a very nice hole, Albert,' she ventured.

'That's because you don't know anything

about growing potatoes,' Mr Grimble told her.

She shook her head. 'No, dear. You're right. What's that at the bottom?'

Everybody looked. Something pink was lying on the floor of the trench, half-hidden by earth. As Skipjack jumped in to pick it up, Mr Grimble spotted the shiny new spade that Oli was holding.

'Where did you get that?' he frowned.

'We could hardly lift your spades,' Oli told him, 'so Reggie lent us his.'

'Did I hear my name?' The friendly window

cleaner appeared again, beaming over the fence.

'I see you're back, Mr G.,' he said cheerfully. 'Fine pair of gardeners you've got there. Hello, Mrs G.! How was choir practice?'

Mrs Grimble blushed. 'Hello, Reggie,' she whispered.

Skipjack had now clambered back out of the trench and was brushing the earth off what looked like a big raspberry.

'Lucky you spotted this, Mrs Grimble. It's my new keyring. It farts.'

'IT DOES WHAT?' boomed Mr Grimble.

'Farts. It's a remote-control farting keyring. I bought it yesterday. It's great. I'll show you how it works . . .'

'You'll do no such thing!' shouted Mr Grimble, nearly blowing Skipjack over. 'You'll stop hanging about and get back to work.'

Mrs Grimble coughed. 'I made you another onion pie this morning, Reggie,' she whispered. 'I'll go and get it.' She pattered into the house. Mr Grimble aimed a final glare at the boys, then the trench and finally the farting keyring and marched away.

'Hey, Skipjack,' called Reggie. 'Let's see that keyring.'

'Sure.' Skipjack chucked the keyring over and Reggie caught it neatly.

'You take out the little bit in the middle,' explained Skipjack, 'and you can put either that bit or the main keyring bit somewhere, and then you press whichever bit you've still got, and the other bit farts. Try it.'

Reggie did as Skipjack instructed, placing the detachable tracker on top of a nearby fence post. Sure enough, it let out a loud and juicy fart.

Reggie roared.

'It's absolutely fantastic!' he exclaimed.

'And useful,' Skipjack pointed out.

'Oh, very useful,' agreed Reggie. 'Especially if you ever buried treasure and had to find it again. Where can I get one?'

'Doctor Levity's joke shop on the High Street,' Skipjack told him. 'Just ask for a Phantom Farter.'

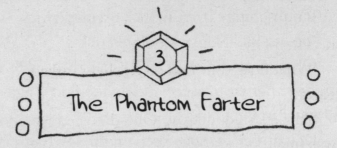

3

The Phantom Farter

Mrs Grimble came out with the onion pie which she handed over the fence to her neighbour. 'There you are, Reggie,' she said, a little breathlessly. 'I made it just the way you like it.'

'Thank you, Mrs G.' Reggie beamed. 'And here's the tin back from yesterday's pie. You're an angel.'

The angel blushed. 'Ooh, Reggie!' she squeaked and, plucking the tin from his hand, she fluttered back indoors.

'I don't suppose you lads would like a lift to the rugby club when you've finished?' called Reggie. 'I'll be popping out for a newspaper anyway.'

The boys gasped. 'In your Morgan?' cried Oli.

'Well, I hardly meant over my shoulder,' grinned Reggie.

'Awesome! Yes please!'

'One day I'm going to have a car like that,' declared Oli.

'What does your dad drive, then?' asked Reggie.

Skipjack said quickly, 'Oli's dad died when he was small.'

Reggie frowned. 'I'm sorry.'

'It's OK,' said Oli.

'He uses mine,' added Skipjack.

Oli phoned his mum, who understood that the chance to ride in a Morgan was a rare treat.

'She wants to meet Reggie first,' he told Skipjack, 'so she's coming here with our rugby stuff in ten minutes. Let's hurry.'

So the boys returned to their digging, spurred on by thoughts of a lift in Reggie's beautiful car, and soon the job was done.

'Hooray!' shouted Skipjack as he tossed out the final clod of earth.

'Bye, Mr Grimble! We've finished!' called Oli, climbing out of the trench. 'Come on, Skip – here's Mum.'

Mrs Biggles handed over the boys' bags,

admired the Morgan and thanked Reggie.

'Don't thank me – I'm having a lovely time,' grinned Reggie. 'I've got five younger brothers at home, just like these two. Ready, boys? Let's go.'

'I'll come and watch you later at the club,' said Oli's mum.

Five seconds later, Oli and Skipjack were sitting together in the back of Reggie's Morgan, more excited than a pair of monkeys in a banana shop. They begged him to put the top down,

despite the fierce January wind that nearly bit off their ears. They wished the rugby club was miles and miles away but in a few short minutes they were there. When they turned into the car park Reggie drove really slowly so that everyone would have time to see them. All boys have a built-in radar system that goes 'ping-pink' when a cool car is in range. By the time the Morgan drew up at the club house an excited throng was clattering across the tarmac in studded boots to

make enthusiastic spluttering noises through mouthguards. Only one boy pretended not to notice: Slugger Stubbins just went on charging at the tackle bags, like an angry rhino practising for the tourist season.

When Oli woke up on Monday morning he felt as if the entire Fiji rugby squad had been using him as a trampoline. He hauled himself out of bed with lots of loud groaning which immediately brought his sister Tara to his doorway.

'Will you be quiet!' she demanded. 'It sounds like *Attack of the Zombies* in here.'

'I have to groan,' groaned Oli. 'I'm in agony.'

'Well, groan quietly, then,' ordered Tara. 'I'm in the middle of training Togo and Pogo and you're frightening them.'

'Who and who?' asked Oli, but Tara was gone. Oli was not very interested in the answer anyway – his sister was a passionate animal rescuer and kept a zoo in their tree house, where all sorts of small creatures hopped, crawled and slid about in jars and cages. Oli went back to his groaning; it somehow made getting up easier.

The species of Tara's trainees was soon
revealed. After Oli had struggled down the Great
North Face of the staircase to the kitchen the
first things he saw on the table were two brown
mice. Tara was feeding them oatflakes. She
looked up when Oli hobbled in.

'Why are you walking in that weird way?' she
asked.

'I told you upstairs. I'm in agony. Why are you
feeding two mice?'

'I told you upstairs – I'm training them.
They're my act. You know, for *Total Talent*.'

The mention of the nation's most popular TV
competition created a stir at the far end of the
breakfast table where Oli's older sister, Becky,
was sheltering from Monday morning behind an
enormous fashion magazine.

'You cannot appear on *Total Talent* with two
brown mice,' Becky declared. 'It would be too
embarrassing.'

'It won't be embarrassing if I win and get to
perform in front of the Queen.'

'But you won't win. Yuck! One of them just
pooed!'

'That shows what he thinks of you,' muttered
Tara. Aloud she said, 'When I get my prize
money, I'll remember not to share any of it with
you. I shall use it *all* for running away to Africa.
So there.'

Oli and Tara's regular cycle route to school took
them past Skipjack's house so they always picked
him up on the way. This morning as usual,
Skipjack was waiting for them on his bike,
leaning against the gatepost at the end of his
drive.

'Hi, Oli! Hi, Tara!' he yelled and fell into line with them. 'Crikey, I was stiff this morning, Oli. I felt like the Frankenstein monster. And I had a horrible nightmare that Mr Grimble was burying me alive.'

'He's a wicked slave-driver,' Oli replied. 'And we've got to get even with him. We need a Plan.'

Skipjack grinned. 'As a matter of fact, Oli my friend, a Plan is exactly what we have.'

'I knew I could count on you, Skip. Let's have a meeting in break.'

'In the art room.'

'Why the art room?' asked Oli.

'Because', said Skipjack mysteriously, 'it's a very artistic plan.'

So, as the school clock struck eleven, Oli Biggles could be seen scampering to the art room, impatient to hear all about Skipjack's Very Artistic Plan. His friend arrived a few moments later, carrying a newspaper.

'I borrowed this from Mr Dodderidge,' he explained. 'He was really pleased. He thought I wanted to read it. I didn't have the heart to tell him we want to cut it up.'

'Why do we want to cut it up?'

'Because we're going to use it to send a message to Mr Grimble,' Skipjack told him. 'I saw this film,' he explained, 'where a bad guy kidnapped a rich guy's dog. And he sent a ransom note asking for lots of money, and the note was made up of letters cut out of newspapers so he didn't leave any clues. See? I've got some paper and an envelope here.' Skipjack plunged a hand into one of his pockets and felt about inside.

Oli was looking doubtful. All of Skipjack's many plans were bonkers but some were brilliantly bonkers and some were badly bonkers and it was often hard to tell which was which. So he asked, 'Did the dog-napper get the ransom money?'

'Well, no,' Skipjack admitted. 'The police caught him.'

'How, if he didn't leave any clues?'

'His neighbours heard barking and got suspicious. He told the police he was barking himself, but no one believed him. So they searched the house, and found the dog. Of course, Mr Grimble doesn't have a dog so we'll have to kidnap something else.'

'We could kidnap Mrs Grimble?' suggested Oli. 'She doesn't bark.'

'As far as we know. But what if he doesn't pay the ransom?'

Oli shuddered. 'We'd have to keep her. And she'd make us eat onion pies. Yuck.'

For a few moments the art room was silent except for the creaking of Skipjack's chair as he rocked it backwards and forwards, deep in thought. Then Oli banged the table, giving his friend such a jolt that his chair legs slid out from under him and he landed on the floor with a clatter.

'Ow!' cried Skipjack. 'What was that for?'

'I've had an awesome idea,' said Oli. 'What about the gnomes!'

'Brilliant!' Skipjack grinned, picking himself up off the floor. 'Gnomes definitely don't bark so they'll make perfect kidnappees.'

'But we're not going to kidnap them for money – we're going to *rescue* them,' Oli told him. 'And set them free!'

This idea pleased Skipjack very much. 'Ha! That'll teach Mr Grimble not to be such a big bully.'

'Here's what we'll do.' Oli counted the tasks on his fingers. 'Number 1 – ask if you can stay the night on Friday. Number 2 – sneak out after lights-out and cycle round to the Grimbles' place and stuff as many gnomes as we can into our backpacks. Number 3 – put our note through the door and scarper. Number 4 – stash the gnomes in the tree house and sneak back to bed.'

'Number 5 – Mr Grimble wakes up on Saturday morning and looks out of the window and there isn't a gnome in sight!' chuckled Skipjack.

'Come on,' said Oli. 'Let's write the note.'

While Skipjack spread the newspaper out on a large table Oli went in search of scissors and glue. He returned to find his friend poring over the front page.

'Look at this,' said Skipjack. 'It's about diamonds.'

POLICE FEAR FOR
BLACK STAR SAFETY!

Sergeant Flower has voiced concerns
about the arrival of the famous Black
Star diamond at the town museum while
the cat-burglar is still at large. This
priceless gem, which is the size of a ping-
pong ball, will be on display from
Thursday for a week, as part of a
collection of jewels belonging to the
Sultana of Kalamistan. Mayor Sir Henry
Widebottom dismissed Sergeant Flower's
fears, saying, 'The Black Star will be
under 24-hour protection by the
museum's team of highly trained guards.
It will be impossible to steal. An exhibit of
this importance will bring prestige to our
town and as your mayor I am very much
in favour of prestige.'

'I always thought a sultana was a female raisin,'
said Oli.

'A very rich raisin,' remarked Skipjack, 'to

have a diamond the size of a ping-pong ball. Of course, you couldn't play ping-pong with a diamond,' he added as he put the scissors to work. 'It wouldn't bounce. Pool, perhaps – golf even, but not ping-pong.'

By the end of break the art room looked as if a blizzard of square snowflakes had swept through, but the message for Mr Grimble and the envelope were finished. Oli read the note aloud:

WE ARE The
GNOME FREEDOM ARMy
We hav ReScued yor
Gnomes From theRe
SLAVeRy. SeRves you Right

Oli folded the letter carefully into its envelope and slipped it in one of the pockets of his school bag.

'Roll on, Friday,' he said with a grin.

4
The Black Star and the Swag-Bagger

The sleepover was granted by the mums and the boys spent every spare moment that week planning their Gnome Freedom Army mission.

Meanwhile excitement was growing across the town over the arrival of the Sultana of Kalamistan's jewels and in particular the magnificent Black Star diamond. When the museum opened its doors on Thursday morning there was a queue of visitors lined up outside. The mayor, Sir Henry Widebottom, stood on the top step and spent ten minutes telling everybody how important he was to have such a famous diamond in his town, before the waiting crowd was finally allowed inside.

Among the many visitors to the exhibition that Thursday there was one who paid particular attention to the position of drainpipes and

windows around the building. The same visitor
calculated the thickness of the security glass in
the Black Star's display cabinet. He took careful
note of the alarm circuit and he found out the
exact number of guards on the duty rota.

On Thursday night the cat-burglar struck
again.

On Friday morning the headline was splashed
across the local paper:

BLACK STAR STOLEN!

Huge reward offered for information leading to recovery of priceless diamond!

'This is completely unexpected,' said the mayor, Sir Henry Widebottom. 'We are dealing with a criminal mastermind.'

Where is the Black Star now?

This same question was on the lips of the whole town but nobody could answer it. Nobody, that is, except Reggie Smith. Reggie knew the answer because the Black Star diamond was sitting on his kitchen table, about to be hidden in a specially adapted garden gnome. For Reggie Smith was not only a window cleaner, he was a world-class cat-burglar. And Mrs Grimble's favourite gnome was not only a gnome, it was an unwitting accomplice in an international diamond-smuggling operation.

Tonight, Reggie would swap the gnome on his kitchen table for its identical twin by the

Grimbles' garden pond, where it would await Saturday-night collection by Reggie's pal Big Ben Baloney. Big Ben was a fence; he found buyers for Reggie's stolen jewels.

Reggie had been stashing his stolen diamonds in the Grimbles' gnomes for about three months now, ever since he had moved to the town and carried out his first robbery there. It tickled him to use a gnome with a black eye-mask and a bag marked SWAG. Little did Mrs Grimble know that Reggie's original gift had been replaced several times over the past twelve weeks, or that Reggie had twenty more upstairs in his bedroom cupboard.

Yes, it had been a good season for Reggie, but soon it would draw to a close. He liked to work in winter, when the evenings were dark and people huddled indoors. Soon the days would be longer and warmer, people would be out and about and Reggie would be off for a holiday in the sun.

But first he had his eye on one more job.

By Friday night, Oli and Skipjack's plan had

been polished until it shone like the lights on Reggie's Morgan. Their dark clothes and biggest backpacks were ready and Oli had even found his Secret Agent moustache. Their bikes were freshly oiled and the alarm clock under Oli's pillow was set for two o'clock. For once they longed for bedtime. They fidgeted and whispered all the way through *Total Talent*, much to the annoyance of Oli's pair of sisters. There was quite a crowd gathered in front of the telly that evening as Tara's mice were watching, too; their trainer wanted them to see what they would be up against.

When at last Oli's mum suggested it was bedtime, Skipjack leapt towards the stairs with such eagerness that she smelt a rat at once.

'Skipjack!' she called. 'Stop right there. Something tells me you boys have a plan for tonight that does not involve lying in bed and sleeping.'

'Really?' asked Skipjack, looking as innocent as a baby lamb.

'Really. Like another midnight feast, for instance?'

'Of course not, Mum,' said Oli. 'Anyway,

Skipjack had so much pizza for supper that even he couldn't possibly eat anything else tonight.'

'Wanna bet?' asked his friend.

Skipjack always slept on a camp bed in Oli's room and by the time Mrs Biggles came up to say goodnight both boys were quietly tucked in. But this fragile illusion of saintliness was shattered when she picked up Skipjack's jeans to fold them over a chair and found, to her surprise, that they rustled heavily.

Skipjack slid quietly under his bedclothes.

Out of the pockets came a chocolate spread and peanut butter sandwich, two bananas, a bag of toffees and half a packet of chocolate chip cookies. Oli sprang to his friend's defence.

'You know what Skipjack's like, Mum – he can't go anywhere without emergency rations.'

'I suppose I should be grateful he didn't pocket the leftover pizza,' sighed his mum.

'I tried,' came a muffled voice from under the duvet, 'but there wasn't room.'

When Mum had gone back downstairs with an armful of food, Skipjack surfaced once more and whispered, 'I think I've been completely brilliant.

If she thinks she's stopped a midnight feast she won't expect us to do anything else tonight.'

'Being completely brilliant by accident doesn't count,' declared Oli. 'Goodnight, Skip.'

'I'm hungry.'

'Go to sleep.'

It seemed only a second later that the alarm was beeping stubbornly, ripping the boys from their peaceful slumbers. Oli sat up and fumbled for his torch, but Skipjack just grunted and rolled over.

'Aw, Mum,' he mumbled. 'Just another five minutes.'

'Time to get up, Skippy-wippy,' whispered Oli,

switching on his torch and shining it on Skipjack's face.

Skipjack opened one eye and used it to glare at Oli. 'My mum does *not* call me Skippy-wippy. She hasn't called me Skippy-wippy for ages. *Nobody* calls me Skippy-wippy and lives, not even you.'

'OK, boss,' chuckled Oli.

The boys had once made a plan of Oli's stairs, marking all the creakiest spots with an 'X'. They had long ago memorised the safest route and now they could get from the top to the bottom, or the bottom to the top, without making a sound. They slipped out through the back door, which Oli locked again behind them before

pocketing the key. Then they cycled away on their Gnome Freedom Army mission.

It was a still, moonless night and the roads were silent and deserted. Street lamps cast dim orange circles at intervals along their route but the Grimbles' garden lay in the shadows between. Here there was just enough pale starlight to pick out the small figures of the gnomes.

The boys set to work, darting from gnome to gnome and putting each one carefully into their backpacks, except the last two, which had to go in Skipjack's bicycle bag. Finally Oli pushed the newspaper note through the Grimbles' front door. The whole operation had taken less than five minutes. Once back at Pond Lane they put the gnomes up in the tree house and soon they were in their beds again, shivering with cold and excitement.

'I wish Mum hadn't found all your food, Skip,' whispered Oli. 'Rescuing gnomes makes you hungry.'

'What about some leftover pizza?' offered Skipjack.

'I thought you couldn't fit that in your pockets?'

'I smuggled it into my wash-bag. Just in case.'

'Skipjack, you're completely brilliant.'

When Oli woke up on Saturday morning the world seemed a bright and shiny place. He grinned. 'I'd give a million pounds to see the look on Mr Grimble's face when he opens that letter.'

'I bet he'll be angrier than the angriest person in Angryland,' chuckled Skipjack. 'If we open the window we might hear him shouting from here.'

Mr Grimble was indeed just breaking the world record for single-handed, long-distance angriness. 'Gnome Freedom Army!' he roared, waving the newspaper-note at his wife. 'How dare they rob us like this!'

'All our little gnomes, gone,' she snivelled.

In short, it is fair to say that the Grimbles were very shocked by this sudden great escape.

But not nearly as shocked as Reggie.

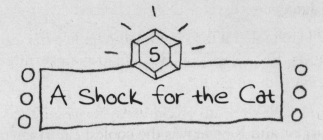

A Shock for the Cat

To understand the depth of Reggie's attachment to the Grimbles' gnomes, it is important to remind ourselves of some key facts. So let's rewind the clock and go over recent events from Reggie's point of view:

On Friday morning, Reggie was sitting at his kitchen table with a nice fat diamond and a cheeky little chap with a swag bag. The rock fitted perfectly into the hole he had made in the gnome's bottom. Reggie sealed this up with clay and chose a quiet moment to swap the naughty gnome with its identical twin perched on a rock by the Grimbles' ornamental pond.

Some time on Saturday night, Reggie's fence Big Ben Baloney would roll up, whip the swag-bag gnome and sell the diamond for Reggie. Early on Sunday morning, Reggie would replace the original gnome.

Except that when Reggie glanced over the fence on Saturday morning, he had a nasty shock. The swag-bag gnome had done a runner, along with all his mates.

You had to have a cool head to be a cat-burglar and Reggie was the coolest cat in town. He quickly saw that there were three possibilities:

Number 1: Big Ben had come early to collect the diamond, forgotten which gnome it was in and taken them all away to be sure he didn't miss it.

Number 2: Mrs Grimble had brought all her little garden friends indoors for some reason. A tea party perhaps, or a nice sing-song – what did he know?

Number 3: All the gnomes, including the swag-bag gnome, had been pinched by person or persons unknown.

If it's 1 or 2, thought Reggie, I'm OK. If it's 3, I'm in trouble.

He went back indoors, picked up the telephone and dialled Big Ben Baloney's number.

''Ello?'' came a voice as deep as a coal mine.

'It's me,' said Reggie in a low voice. 'Have you got it?'

'Got what?'

Reggie clicked his tongue impatiently. Big Ben was a useful partner to have in the criminal underworld as he looked like a distant cousin of Mount Everest but sometimes Reggie was sure that his brain was also made of solid rock.

'The item for collection,' he explained through gritted teeth.

'Oh, you mean the diamond!' boomed Big Ben.

'Shh!'

'Sorry, Reg. No, I 'aven't got it yet. I'm coming tonight, like we agreed. Why? 'As something 'appened?'

'It looks like it. Don't come unless I call again.'
Reggie hung up. This was not looking good. He
decided to go round to the Grimbles and make
sympathetic noises. He might find something out.

The kitchen door was opened by a very tearful
Mrs Grimble.

'Oh, Reggie,' she sniffed, 'all my little gnomes
have gone.' She dabbed her red nose and blotchy
eyes with a scrumple of tissue.

Reggie's heart sank. So it was Possibility
Number 3 after all – removal by person or
persons unknown. 'Dear oh dear,' he cooed.
'Who can have taken them, I wonder?'

'We know exactly who took them,' sobbed Mrs
Grimble.

Reggie brightened. 'You do? That's great!'

'It was the Gnome Freedom Army,' wailed Mrs
Grimble. 'We had a note. Albert's just calling the
police. Are you all right, Reggie?'

Reggie had started violently at the word
'police' – he liked to keep as far away as possible
from this variety of human being. Oli's friend
Skipjack felt exactly the same way about science
teachers.

Through the door to the hall he could hear Mr Grimble roaring down the telephone: 'What do you mean, not an emergency? This is a major crime scene – why can you only send one constable? All the others are out looking for the diamond? Call this a police service? I'm a tax-payer I am . . .'

They heard the telephone being slammed down. Mrs Grimble winced.

'I'd better go,' muttered Reggie. 'I don't want to get in the way of the constable. Cheer up, Mrs G. Tell you what – I happen to have another gnome just like the one I gave you. I'll pop over later with it. Bye, now.'

'Goodbye, Reggie,' whispered Mrs Grimble. 'Thank you for your kind words at our time of loss.'

It was a thoughtful Reggie who vaulted back over the fence. If the police found the gnomes, they might discover the Black Star. He'd been careful with fingerprints, but explaining how the diamond found its way inside the very gnome that he had given Mrs Grimble would be tricky. He wondered about the Gnome Freedom Army.

He suspected it was just a couple of kids having a laugh, in which case the diamond would be safe as long as they didn't use the gnomes as footballs. He just had to get to it before the police did.

The Gnome Freedom Army, meanwhile, was in its headquarters (the tree house) admiring the haul from its first campaign. The eleven liberated gnomes were all – nearly all – smiling up at the boys with heart-warming gratitude.

'I used to think gnomes were a bit creepy,' mused Oli, 'but I'm getting to quite like them.'

Skipjack gave the nearest gnome a pat on the head. 'Don't worry, guys,' he said. 'You'll never have to slave for that gorilla again. My favourite', he added, standing up and pointing, 'is that one over there, with the eye-mask and the swag-bag. I bet he's a bundle of trouble.'

There came the sound of footsteps up the ladder and Tara's head popped up through the door.

'Uh-oh, talking of trouble . . .' remarked Oli, as his sister eyed the gnomes.

Sure enough: 'What are those?' demanded Tara.

'They're refugees,' said Oli.

'You're not keeping them here?'

'Wrong.'

'But you can't!'

'Wrong again.'

'They'll have to pay rent.'

'Rent?'

'To stay here. I want to train Togo and Pogo up here and your gnomes –'

'Refugees,' corrected Skipjack, but Tara ignored him.

'– are taking up too much space.'

'But you've got the whole house to train your mice in,' said Oli.

Tara sighed deeply. 'They have to get used to lots of different surroundings, of course. Otherwise they'll be really nervous when I take them to *Total Talent* and they'll get stage fright or something.'

'But I don't charge rent to all your frogs and newts and jars of slimy crawly things,' objected Oli, waving an arm at the shelves full of Tara's zoo. 'Why should the gnomes –'

'Refugees,' whispered Skipjack.

'Why should they –'

'Shh!' interrupted Skipjack and he cocked his head on one side like a dog. 'Voices!' he whispered. They all crept to the window and peeped out.

On the front doorstep stood Mr Grimble. Everyone quickly ducked.

'All my gnomes!' Mr Grimble was shouting. 'Every single one!'

'Terrible for you, I'm sure,' said Mrs Biggles very calmly, 'but I still don't see why you're telling me.'

'Because your boy and his friend were in our garden last Sunday. They knew we had gnomes. The policeman said the gang was probably quite young, on account of the small footprints . . .'

There was silence.

'What's happening?' demanded Skipjack, crouched below the window.

Oli inched upwards for a cautious peep. 'Mum's giving him another one of her Cold Looks,' he whispered. Skipjack shivered.

Then they heard Mrs Biggles's voice. 'Mr Grimble, there must be dozens of boys – and girls – in this town with the same size feet. Just because Oli and Skipjack put a silly poster in your bus gives you no right to accuse them of running off with your gnomes. Next you'll say they've got the Black Star diamond, too! Now kindly leave us alone. Goodbye.'

The front door closed and Oli ducked again as Mr Grimble turned to leave. When the coast was clear he exclaimed, 'Well done, Mum!'

'She was awesome,' agreed Skipjack. 'I wish I could do a Cold Look like that.'

'The problem is', frowned Oli, 'that Mr Grimble will go on suspecting us, whatever Mum says.'

'Well, there's a simple way to stop him,' said Skipjack with a shrug. 'We must rescue gnomes from other people's gardens, too. Then he'll have no more reason to think it's us.'

'Good idea,' agreed Oli. 'We'll hide them up here till Saturday and then we'll set them free in the park.'

'That's not allowed,' Tara told them. 'You'll get into trouble.'

'Oh no, we won't,' said Oli. ''Cos no one will find out. Anyway, we're not *stealing*, not like the cat-burglar.'

'We're *rescuing*,' explained Skipjack, 'which is completely different.'

'Completely,' agreed Oli. 'It's not as if we want to keep the gnomes. We just want to help them, and teach Mr Grimble a lesson at the same time.'

'I want 10p a day for every gnome,'

announced Tara.

Oli swung round on her. 'For the last time, I am not paying you rent!'

'Who said anything about rent?' said Tara coolly. 'I want silence money.'

'That's blackmail!'

'It's for a good cause,' Tara pointed out. 'I can add it to my Africa money.'

Oli glared at her. 'If it gets you to Timbuktu any quicker, it's DEFINITELY a good cause.'

Now that more rescues were planned, the GFA had lots of work to do. To begin with, more newspaper messages would be needed, so Oli and Skipjack spent every spare minute of Monday and Tuesday making a mess in the art room. Mr Dodderidge was delighted by Skipjack's new interest in current affairs and donated his newspapers gladly, little guessing that he was aiding a secret mission.

The boys made long detours on their way to and from school, during which they peered over walls and hedges in search of gnomes. They ruled out gardens in busy streets and those with dog kennels and they also ruled out the meagre strip of flowers in front of Sergeant Flower's police station, where an old, chipped gnome fished in a mossy bird bath.

'Anyway, I like Sergeant Flower,' declared Oli. 'He plays rugby.'

By Tuesday evening they were ready, with a list of addresses and a sheaf of messages. They had decided to operate separately for added speed and because, it being the middle of the week, there was no chance of a sleepover. Each boy would have to creep out of his own house, do his daring deeds and creep back in again.

'Good luck, Skip,' said Oli as they parted at his gate.

'Good luck, Oli,' replied Skipjack. 'If I get caught, I won't give you away, not even if they pull all my fingernails out one by one.'

'That's good to know, Skip. Me neither. Not even if they force-feed me with onion pie.'

'You're a brave man, Oli.'

They shook hands solemnly and Skipjack cycled home.

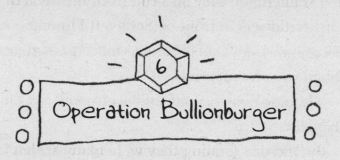

6 Operation Bullionburger

By Thursday morning it was standing room only
in the tree house, where the gnomes were
huddled together like penguins on an ice floe.
Skipjack had popped round before school to add
his to the flock and the boys were congratulating
themselves on missions accomplished, while Tara
counted the refugees and multiplied them by
10p.

'On Saturday we'll take them all to the park,'
said Oli. 'Tara can help.'

'No, she can't,' said Tara. 'Togo and Pogo
need more training. They still can't roll over and
it's only three days to our *Total Talent* audition.'

But Oli, boosted by the success of the Great
Gnome Rescue, was in no mood to take any
nonsense from Tara. 'If you want your money,'
he told her, 'you'll help.'

Tara's chin rose. 'You seem to have forgotten, Oli, that if you *don't* pay me, I'll tell Mum about the gnomes. And she'll have to tell Mr Grimble that it was you after all.'

'Shouldn't we just pay up?' whispered Skipjack.

But Oli was fed up of being held to ransom by his little sister. 'Go on then,' he said, 'Tell Mum. Wave goodbye to all those 10p's.'

'Eek!' This was Skipjack.

Tara glared at her brother.

'All right, I'll help,' she said crossly, 'but I think you're really mean.'

'You shouldn't try to blackmail your own brother,' Oli told her firmly.

'Phew,' said Skipjack. 'Can we go to school now, please?'

On their way they passed the local newsagent's and Skipjack nearly crashed his bike when he saw the headline on a newspaper board outside:

GNOMES DISAPPEAR!

'Look!' he shouted. 'We're famous!'

'Cool!' cried Oli. 'Let's get a paper. Who's got money?' He looked hopefully at his sister.

'Ha! If I had a squillion pounds I wouldn't give you any.'

'My mum and dad get their papers from this shop,' said Skipjack. 'Perhaps I can get one on their account.'

He popped inside the shop and came out a minute later waving the newspaper triumphantly. They read the front page:

GNOME FREEDOM ARMY STRIKES!

The local crime wave continues with the theft of dozens of garden gnomes by a gang calling itself the Gnome Freedom Army.

Operating in the dead of night, the soldiers of the GFA remove gnomes with stealth and cunning and leave messages accusing householders of keeping gnomes in slavery.

No gnome is safe!

> Meanwhile the police are no closer to finding the Black Star diamond or the mystery cat-burglar.

'"Stealth and cunning",' quoted Skipjack happily. 'That describes us perfectly.'

'Come on, soldier of the GFA,' grinned Oli as he rolled up the newspaper and shoved it into his friend's backpack. 'Let's go to school.'

They were just turning in at the school gates when a huge black car with smoked-glass windows roared past, nearly knocking them off their bikes.

'Here comes the President of the World,' said Oli. 'Oh no, it's only Nevis.'

The car screeched to a halt and ejected a short, dumpy boy with a face like a toad. Nevis Bullionburger was a recent arrival at the school, but already everyone knew that his father, Mr Lucrus P. Bullionburger, was extremely rich. This was because Nevis told everyone he was. Anything anyone had, Nevis had too, only Nevis's was bigger. Oli and Skipjack still chuckled about the time they had caught Nevis out with a

carefully prepared trap which went like this:

Oli: I've got a surround sound cinema in my bedroom.

Nevis: Me too. Bet mine's bigger than yours.

Oli: I've also got my very own quad bike with a 100cc engine.

Nevis: Me too. Bet mine's bigger than yours.

Skipjack: I've got a rocket-fuelled bottom at the top of my legs.

Nevis: Me too. Bet mine's bigger –

He stopped.

Oli: Sorry, Nevis? You were saying?

Nevis scowled, while Oli and Skipjack laughed till they cried.

On this particular morning, the whole school was talking about gnomes and diamonds. Nevis Bullionburger, of course, not only had hundreds of diamonds in his safe that were all much bigger than the Black Star, but also a gnome by his pond that was ten times the size of every other gnome in the town.

'You know what we've got to do,' muttered Oli in Skipjack's ear.

'One final mission for the GFA,' agreed Skipjack.

'Tomorrow night. Get it?'

'Got it.'

'Good.'

On Friday morning the boys were pleased to see that the Gnome Freedom Army had once again made the headlines:

MORE GNOMES GO!

Gnome-owners are taking action against the Gnome Freedom Army. Bus driver Albert Grimble, an early victim, has formed a Gnome Guard, saying, 'We cannot depend on the police. It is up to

citizens to protect themselves.' Captain
Grimble and his Gnome Guard comrades
will be patrolling the streets of our town
with garden rakes at the ready. Details of
how to join, and how to make your own
trap for the GFA by attaching trip wires
to your wind chime, can be found on
page 4.

The boys chose 8 p.m. as the best time for
Operation Bullionburger. They figured that any
house as stuffed with diamonds and other loot as
Nevis claimed his house was stuffed would have a
major security system, both inside and out. So it
would be safest to visit while the occupants were
still up and about, and before all these alarms
were switched on. Also, 8 p.m. was *Total Talent*-
o'clock, which made it not only the easiest time
to slip out of Oli's house but also, the boys
hoped, the safest time to slip into the
Bullionburgers' garden.

'Because they'll all be watching telly, just like
everyone else,' said Skipjack.

'On their mega-screen digital interactive

20:00 hours

20:00 hours

super-definition cinema centre,' added Oli.

'That's the one.'

And so at eight o'clock that evening the soldiers of the Gnome Freedom Army set forth on their final mission: to liberate the Bullionburger gnome.

Also at eight o'clock that evening, cat-burglar Reggie Smith set forth on his final mission: to liberate the Bullionburger diamonds.

The Gnome Freedom Army went by bike, keeping a sharp lookout for the Gnome Guard.

20:04 hours

Reggie Smith went on foot, keeping a sharp lookout for everyone.

At 8.04, Oli and Skipjack arrived at the huge electric gates of the Bullionburger mansion and skirted the wall to the south.

At 8.06, Reggie arrived at the huge electric gates of the Bullionburger mansion and skirted the wall to the north.

Oli looked up at the high, smooth wall. 'This is a saddles job,' he said. 'And we'll need a climbing tree on the inside so we can get back out.'

They came to a spot where a likely-looking tree grew close to the other side of the wall, with a couple of overhanging branches. Then they parked the bikes against the wall, pressing them firmly down into the grass, and carefully climbed up them until they were standing on the saddles.

They peeked over the wall.

'What if Nevis's dad isn't a fan of *Total Talent* and is out there somewhere with his rake?' whispered Skipjack.

They paused for a few moments of hard listening and then, having heard nothing but silence, they hauled themselves on to the wall and jumped down on the inside.

'Nevis said the gnome was by the pond,' whispered Oli. 'So first we have to find the pond.'

'We could call the fish,' suggested Skipjack. 'Here, fishy fishies . . .'

'Skipjack.'

'Yes, Oli?'

'You're crazy.'

'Shh, I can hear them blowing bubbles. This way.'

Reggie, meanwhile, had popped over the wall, darted silently through the garden and was now scaling the house. He climbed with the speed and effortless grace of a salamander. He was aiming for the end window on the top floor because he knew, from cautious snoops during window-cleaning jobs, that in this room was a cupboard housing a safe. When he reached the window, he took out his glass-cutter and made a hole big enough for his hand. Then he reached in, undid the clasp and pushed open the window.

Skipjack led the way through an orchard and Oli, who did not want to shout after him, had no choice but to follow.

On the other side of the orchard was a clipped hedge with an archway in the middle and on the other side of the hedge was a green expanse of perfectly smooth lawn. In the centre of the lawn was a collection of bushes clustered around . . . a fish pond.

'There you are,' said Skipjack proudly.

It was of course an Olympic-sized fish pond, oblong and enclosed by a low wall. In the centre, marooned on a raised sundial, stood the most enormous gnome the boys had ever seen.

'It's a monster gnome,' whispered Oli.

'It's a Bullionburger gnome,' Skipjack pointed out.

'Question is: will it fit in my backpack?'

'Question is: did you remember your snorkel?'

'How come it's me going in?'

'Because I can't swim.'

'You won't have to swim, you wally. It's only knee-deep.'

'We could toss. I've got a coin somewhere.

Here it is. Heads I win, tails you lose.'

Oli gave up. 'OK, OK, I'll do it.' He clambered over the wall into the dark water and gasped. 'Cold!' he squeaked.

'Be brave, Oli,' said Skipjack helpfully. 'Hey, is that a piranha over there, hiding under that leaf?'

'Skipjack!'

'Sorry. False alarm. It's just a vampire goldfish.'

'Just keep a lookout, will you?' urged Oli through chattering teeth.

Luckily for the various intruders who were busy removing the Bullionburgers' property, all three members of the family were cocooned in their home cinema, weighing up the talents of Zepp and his Yodelling Sausage Dog against those of Yakimodo the Human Yo-Yo.

Two floors above them, Reggie had opened a safe the size of the national bank vault and was scooping its glittering contents into a drawstring bag tied to his belt.

Meanwhile the fearless pond-wader reached the sundial, picked up the giant statue and

placed the very last Gnome Freedom
Army letter in its place before turning
to wade back.

'Careful,' he whispered as he
handed the gnome to Skipjack. 'It
weighs a ton.' He climbed over the
wall again, glad to be out of the
freezing water, and together they
stuffed the gnome into the backpack.

Then, as Oli stood up to swing the
backpack on, he happened to glance
up at the house. What he saw made
him freeze.

Abseiling down the side of the
house was the dark figure of a man.

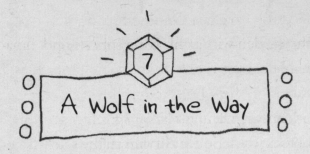

7
A Wolf in the Way

'What's wrong?' asked Skipjack, seeing his friend's horrified face.

'Someone climbing down the wall,' hissed Oli. 'It must be the cat-burglar! Quick – hide!' He grabbed Skipjack and hauled him behind the nearest clump of bushes.

'Let's see!' Skipjack popped his head up over the leaves. 'Wow, look at him go! I wonder what he's pinched.' Then he ducked. 'He's coming this way,' he whispered. The two boys pressed themselves deeper into the bush and held their breath. They caught a fleeting glimpse of a silent black figure before it melted into the night.

'Let's give him a minute and then we'll leg it,' said Oli.

But suddenly the deafening clang of alarm bells filled the air. Powerful beams flashed on, flooding the garden with light. For a split second, horror held the boys rooted to the spot. Then they ran.

Among Oli and Skipjack's many sporting heroes was a South African rugby star who was famous for racing against a cheetah. But if this speedy pair had been pitched against the Gnome Freedom Army in a sprint to the Bullionburgers' garden wall, the rugby hero and his cat would have screeched to a halt and watched with awe the scorching pace of Oli and Skipjack.

When the boys reached the wall they threw themselves at the tree which they had earlier pinpointed as their escape route. Numb to the grazes and scratches of the jagged bark and spiky twigs, they scrambled up to an overhanging branch and shuffled along it until they could climb on to the wall. Then they dropped to the ground, grabbed their bikes and took off like bullets, whizzing all the way back to Oli's house. Finally, safe behind the garden shed, they collapsed on to the grass, their muscles burning and their chests heaving.

When at last he had enough breath to talk, Oli said, 'Well, that's the end of my life as a freedom fighter. Rescuing gnomes is getting much too scary.'

'It was all that burglar's fault,' said Skipjack. 'We weren't even moving when those alarms went off. Pretty useless cat-burglar if you ask me. Ouch: that evil tree – it nearly tore my whole leg off.' He felt the side of his leg gently and then sat up.

'My trousers! They're torn to bits!'

'Wow, that's some rip,' said Oli, impressed. 'From top to bottom. Air conditioning.'

'My leg's been ripped from top to bottom, too,' grumbled Skipjack. 'Even my pocket's been ripped.' A sudden look of alarm spread over Skipjack's face. He clutched at what was left of the shredded trouser pocket. Then he plunged his hand into his other pocket and felt about frantically. Then he looked at Oli.

'My Phantom Farter keyring – it's gone,' he squeaked.

Oli sat up. 'Are you sure it was in your pocket?'

'Positive. Look, here's the little tracker from my other pocket. The keyring must have fallen out when my trousers were ripped in that tree. What if Nevis finds it and recognises it and shows it to his dad? Nevis says his dad's much bigger than everyone else's dad . . .' Skipjack gulped.

'Calm down, Skip,' said Oli. 'They can't prove it's yours. Are you missing anything else – anything that might give you away?'

Skipjack went rather pink. 'I think I might have had a little list of girlfriends in the same pocket,' he mumbled.

'In code?'

'I blogging well hope so. Getting shouted at by Nevis's dad will be bad enough, without everyone knowing who my girlfriends are. Even my girlfriends don't know who they are.'

'That's the best way,' said Oli, wisely. He
patted his friend on the back. 'Don't worry, Skip.
They could just have fallen out on the way home.
We'll look for them in the morning.'

DOUBLE BULLIONBURGER ROBBERY!

In a daring raid on Mr Lucrus P.
Bullionburger's mansion last night, the
entire contents of his safe were stolen,
including his priceless collection of
diamond-encrusted, solid gold Monopoly
pieces. The bold theft bears all the
acrobatic hallmarks of the Cat-Burglar,
but in a strange twist, a super-sized
garden gnome was also taken by the
Gnome Freedom Army.

It was Saturday morning and the boys were
standing outside the newsagent with a copy of the
morning paper.

'To think how close we came to seeing who
the cat-burglar is,' said Oli, squashing the
newspaper into his jacket pocket. 'We might
have collected the reward for helping to

find the Black Star diamond.'

'At least there's nothing in the paper about the Phantom Farter or my list of girlfriends,' Skipjack said.

'See? We'll probably find them in the road somewhere. Let's go and look.'

So the boys traced their route back to the Bullionburgers', but there was no sign of the list or the keyring.

There was, however, a shiny new notice on the Bullionburgers' gate:

WARNING: GUARD DOG ON PATROL

'I don't believe they've got a guard dog,' scoffed Skipjack, peering through the gates. 'I think they're just pretending, to stop anyone else robbing them. If they do have a guard dog, why isn't it here, guarding?'

As if in answer, a huge hound appeared out of nowhere and hurled itself at the gates, gnashing its teeth. It had wild yellow eyes, a Mohican of raised hackles down its spine and fangs like bananas. Skipjack sprang away with his hair on end.

'That's not a dog, it's a wolf,' he shouted over
the barrage of barks.

'Yeah, and he wants you for breakfast, Skip.'

'Well, I'm not on the menu. He can go and eat
Nevis instead.'

The boys left the wolf and circled the wall
until they reached the trouser-slashing tree. Here
they made a thorough search, but the area was

entirely empty of Phantom Farters and cryptic lists.

'I knew it,' sighed Skipjack. He took the small tracker out of his pocket and pressed it.

From the other side of the wall came a rich, juicy fart.

Skipjack groaned. 'If I go over, I'll be eaten by the wolf. If I don't go over and they find the Phantom Farter, I'll be punished by Mr Bullionburger. Just think how big *his* potato trench would have to be.'

'Skip, don't panic,' urged Oli.

But it was too late: Skipjack was panicking. 'What if they think I'm the cat-burglar, too?' he wailed.

Oli mentally compared the lithe, silent figure skimming down the wall with Skipjack, who could hardly climb on to a chair without falling off and breaking something.

'Trust me, Skip. They won't.'

'They might, and then they'll tell the police and then I'll go to prison. And even *worse*, if they find the list and crack our code, they'll know that ALL those girlfriends are mine!' Skipjack collapsed against the wall in a boneless heap of gloom.

Oli sighed, lost for comforting words. Then he had an idea. 'Come on,' he said and hauled his friend to his feet.

'Where to?' asked Skipjack.

'Sid's place,' said Oli. 'Sid will cheer you up.'

The boys had first met Sid during Oli's entanglement with a Mum Shop that had once done business in the town. She had become a good friend; their only friend, indeed, who could be trusted with such a secret as this and also the only one who ran a pizza shop, where she made the best triple-pepperoni pizzas in the whole town. She was big, bright and bouncy with a mad mop of orange hair. Oli was confident that Sid would sympathise with the struggles of the Gnome Freedom Army and help to retrieve the Phantom Farter.

Mrs Happy's Pizza Shop was not yet open when the boys arrived, but a couple of knocks brought Sid from the kitchen to the front door. She beamed when she saw her visitors and hurried to let them in.

'Hiya, Oli! Hiya, Skip! It's smashing to see you guys!' She slapped them heartily on the back with the force of a demolition ball. 'How's life?'

'To tell the truth,' said Oli, 'we're in a spot of trouble.'

'Big spot or little spot?' asked Sid cheerfully, pulling out a couple of bar stools for them to sit on. The boys hoisted themselves up.

'Big,' sighed Skipjack.

'Approaching Awesome,' added Oli.

'Ah. What kind of trouble?' asked Sid, as she poured them each a big, icy Cola.

Skipjack counted the categories on his fingers. 'Gnome trouble, Phantom Farter trouble, list-of-girlfriends trouble and now maybe diamond trouble as well.' He turned to Oli. 'Can you think of any more?'

Oli shook his head. 'Only Grimble trouble. But we're always in Grimble trouble so that hardly counts.'

Sid chuckled. 'Even by your standards, guys, that's a lot of trouble. You'd better tell me all about it.'

So they did.

When they had finished Sid nodded
thoughtfully. 'I see what you mean,' she said.
'You are both in big trouble. Not awesome yet,
but big. You see, what you've done is illegal.'

A Triple-Pepperoni Plan

The word 'illegal' was followed by a long silence and then a double gulp.

'Illegal?' repeated Oli. 'You mean, like a crime? Like stealing?'

Sid nodded. 'It was a crime, Oli. It was stealing, too. Taking other people's things is always a no-no.'

'Even gnomes?' asked Skipjack.

'Even gnomes,' Sid told him.

'Even from mean old Mr Grimble and nasty little Nevis?' asked Oli.

'Even from them. Jolly tempting, I agree, but a no-no.'

'Then they *will* lock us up!' squeaked Skipjack. 'With poisoners and mad axe-men!'

'What can we do, Sid?' asked Oli, trying to push from his mind a vision of Skipjack and him

in striped pyjamas, chained together and surrounded by wild-eyed murderers.

'Well, you have to return all the gnomes,' Sid told them. 'As soon as possible, and pay for any broken ones.'

'There aren't any broken ones,' protested Skipjack, looking shocked at the very idea.

'We've been really careful with them,' said Oli. 'Skipjack talks to them every day. But we can't remember whose is whose. We were going to set them all free in the park this afternoon.'

'In the Wild Garden,' added Skipjack, ''cos no one ever goes there.'

Sid pondered this. Finally she said, 'You could set them free and I could be watching out for you from a bench somewhere and then I could "find" them straight away and tell the police. Then they would all be taken to the station and the owners could collect them from there.'

'That's a great idea,' said Oli, relieved. 'We've got so many we'll need to make two journeys, so you must wait till we've been and gone twice before you go and find them.'

'Smashing,' said Sid.

But Skipjack sighed. 'Half of me says "phew", but the other half is really sad to think that all Mr Grimble's poor gnomes will have to go back.'

'Well, I'm sure the Gnome Freedom Army has taught him a lesson,' chuckled Sid. 'He'll be very nice to them now.'

'Plus there's still the problem of the Phantom Farter,' said Skipjack dolefully. 'Nevis will guess it's mine and then they might think I'm the *cat-burglar* instead. Then they'll lock me up for sure.'

Oli suspected that if it wasn't for the looming threat of prison, Skipjack would rather like people to think he was a world-class jewel thief.

'Just how fierce was this guard dog?' asked Sid.

'On a scale of one to ten,' reflected Oli, 'I'd say about seventy-five.'

'I see. So nipping over the wall again is out of the question?'

'Definitely,' said Skipjack. 'I value my life and all my limbs.'

'In that case your only chance is for one of you to go in through the gates like a normal visitor,' said Sid. 'Then they'll tie the dog up somewhere and the other one of you can pop over the wall and get the keyring.'

'But who would we visit?' asked Oli.

'Nevis, of course,' replied Sid. 'You'll have to make friends with Nevis.'

Skipjack was struck dumb by the hideous choice of spending years behind bars with a horde of dangerous villains, or sucking up to the awesomely awful Nevis Bullionburger. What a choice! He looked so miserable that Sid's big heart went out to him.

'I know just the thing to perk you up, young Skipjack,' she beamed. 'I'll make you both a nice big triple-pepperoni pizza with extra cheese!'

She bustled off to the kitchen. Pizza is the answer to every problem, she thought as she threw one together with skilful speed. Suddenly she slapped her hand to her forehead and cried, 'That's it!' She popped the pizza into the oven and hurried back to the boys.

'I've had a smashing idea,' she exclaimed.

'What?' asked the boys.

'Well, when I had a job with the Ping Yong police, there was a really nasty thief at work called Fling Flung. We knew where he lived but we could never get to him, 'cos he had a pair of massively scary guard dogs. Then one day we came up with a plan: I kept the dogs busy by feeding them titbits through the gate while my partner nipped over the fence. He caught Fling Flung red-handed, counting up all his stolen money.'

'What did you feed them with?' Skipjack wanted to know.

'Sweet and sour prawn balls,' Sid told him.

'Yum,' said Skipjack, licking his lips.

'But we'll use pizza,' continued Sid.

Oli grinned. 'I knew you'd think of something, Sid.'

'Ask your mums if you can stay here tonight,' Sid told them. 'Then come back this evening with your toothbrush, a sleeping bag and a good bit of rope and we'll go out after dark and get the Phantom Farter.'

When Oli and Skipjack left Sid's pizza shop after their mid-morning snack, life was looking bright again. Sid had promised to be on her park bench from three o'clock, so the boys agreed to meet in the tree house after lunch to pack up the first load of gnomes.

As Oli cycled home, he hoped his sister would remember her promise to help them take the gnomes to the Wild Garden.

He found Tara in her bedroom, glaring at her mice.

'They *still* won't roll over properly,' she huffed. 'They've only scored two out of ten so far and the *Total Talent* audition is tomorrow.'

Oli shrugged. 'Perhaps they just prefer being right way up. Anyway, they look knackered, and dizzy. Why not give them a rest? You can have your lunch and then come to the park and earn lots of money.'

'All right,' sighed Tara. 'But I'm not helping because I care about you or your silly refugees. I'm only helping because I want to run away to Africa.'

When they reached the park the boys looked round for Sid and soon spotted her on a distant bench, with a newspaper. She gave them a wave disguised as a stretch.

The so-called Wild Garden was in a fenced-off corner of the park and was in fact less like a jungly bit of Borneo and more like a scruffy patch of long grass and bushes – a kind of holiday camp for sparrows and hedgehogs. Tara stood on guard near the gate while Oli and Skipjack slipped inside with the bulging backpacks. The boys had been gone for about five minutes, and Tara was picking the leaves off a twig and wondering, in a bored way, if they had been eaten by a lion, when she happened to glance up. Marching along the path towards her was a policeman. Far away she could see Sid jumping up and down on her bench, pointing and waving frantically.

'Good afternoon,' said the policeman briskly as he passed.

For a second Tara froze. Then she shook herself and shouted, 'Stop! Where are you going?'

The policeman paused with his hand on the Wild Garden gate and turned round, surprised and not altogether pleased by this sudden interrogation from a ten-year-old girl.

'Police business, miss.' He pushed open the gate but she leapt in front of him and pulled it closed again. 'You can't go in there!' she announced firmly.

The policeman frowned. He had not joined the force so that other people could tell him what to do.

'Move away, miss,' he said in a tone so heavy with warning that 'or else . . .' was unnecessary.

Inside the Wild Garden, Skipjack had rejected one spot after another as not cosy or safe enough for the gnomes and Oli was fighting the urge to jump up and down screaming and tearing his hair out.

'We must leave them somewhere nice,' Skipjack insisted.

'But there isn't anywhere else!' exclaimed Oli.

Happily Skipjack found a big tree which he declared would be very nice, so that was where the gnomes were placed, in a large ring.

'They look so happy to be free,' mused Skipjack as he put down his last gnome and gave it a pat. 'Good luck, little fellow.' He sighed. 'I'm going to miss those gnomes.'

'I'll buy you one for your birthday,' promised
Oli. 'Come on – let's go home for the rest.'

But as they neared the gate, still concealed by
shrubs and bushes, they heard Tara's voice
saying loudly, 'What I mean is . . . you can't go in
there because . . . because . . . I've lost my kitten.'

The boys stopped in their tracks.

'And I think it's near the pond,' continued
Tara quickly, 'because of the fish and I'm really
worried that it might drown so please will you

come with me right now and look for it?'

The next voice they heard explained everything.

'Sorry, miss, but I have urgent police business in this garden. We are searching in all likely locations for the missing gnomes.'

Oli and Skipjack glanced at one another in alarm, for the situation looked tricky. Behind them rose the park wall, topped with iron spikes. Around them lay a garden which was not nearly wild enough to hide them from a determined searcher. In front of them ran a fence which they could not hope to cross without being spotted by Tara's policeman, who sounded like a *very* determined searcher. Oli looked up. If only they could fly.

But his little sister was a fighter.

'I saw lots of gnomes,' she told the policeman, 'in the long grass by the tennis courts. Dozens of them. I was there a minute ago, looking for my kitten, the one you won't help me find that's about to drown in the pond.'

'Right,' said the policeman stiffly, 'I'll check there first,' and he hurried away.

The boys burst out of the undergrowth.

'You were great, Tara! Gimme five!'

'We'll give you a pay rise!'

In the distance, Sid had collapsed on her bench and was fanning herself with her newspaper.

'Quick,' said Oli. 'Let's go and get the others!'

But when they returned to the park for the second time they spotted a black figure prowling about the Wild Garden: Tara's policemen had beaten them to it.

Sid was pacing circles around her bench and beckoned urgently. They went over.

'He came back straight after you'd gone and found the gnomes,' she hissed. 'You must go away quickly, especially Tara. We'll talk tonight.'

Later that afternoon, while Sergeant Flower lined up the Wild Garden gnomes on his counter to examine them for clues, Reggie was in his kitchen, sealing up the bottom of yet another swag-bagger. As he worked, he thought about the gnome containing the Black Star diamond, which the Gnome Freedom Army had taken in their raid on the Grimbles, and he wondered for the thousandth time where that gnome was now.

This new gnome contained not diamonds, but a coded note to Reggie's fence, Big Ben Baloney, who was due to come tonight to collect the Bullionburger diamonds. For some reason Big Ben wasn't answering his phone, so Reggie had no way of telling him that stashing the sparklers in the gnomes was getting a bit risky. But if Big Ben found no gnome to collect, he would probably come straight to Reggie's door and bang on it loudly, because he had granite in his head instead of a brain.

So Reggie had made a plan. He would hide the Bullionburger diamonds in a temporary, but safe place. Then he would swap this new gnome for the one he had given Mrs Grimble after the raid. Big Ben would come along, collect the gnome and find the coded message which would explain the situation. Reggie planned to watch the gnome like a hawk all night, so that if the pesky Gnome Freedom Army turned up to pinch it he could follow them and find the Black Star.

A Crowded Night

Saturday's moon rose high in the sky on its nightly stroll through the heavens. It shone down on the peaceful faces of Oli and Skipjack, who were snuggled up in their sleeping bags in Sid's flat above the pizza shop. It illuminated the vigilant figure of Reggie, as he sat at his window watching over the swag-bag gnome. It also cast silvery beams on the burly form of Mr Albert Grimble as he set out with his trusty rake to lead the night patrol of the Gnome Guard. Reggie watched with a wry smile as Mr Grimble marched away, for little did his neighbour know that the one place he should really be keeping an eye on tonight was his own front garden.

The moon even shone a fleeting spotlight on the hairy shape of the Bullionburger hound going in and out of the bushes after rabbity smells, and it sparkled through the police-station window on the buttons of Sergeant Flower's uniform, as that stout officer of the law answered the desk telephone.

'Police station,' muttered Sergeant Flower, stirring a third spoonful of sugar into his steaming mug of tea.

'Ah, good,' said a stuffy voice. 'It's the mayor here.'

Sergeant Flower rolled his eyes. 'Good evening, Sir Henry,' he sighed.

'I'm very worried about all these robberies,' said the mayor. 'Everybody's blaming me and it's not fair. I can't sleep.'

'Would you like me to sing you a lullaby, Sir Henry?'

'No, I would not,' said the mayor told him crossly. 'I want you out patrolling the streets, not sitting behind your desk with a nice cuppa.'

Sergeant Flower looked around, startled. How did he know?

'There might be hordes of robbers out stealing things this very moment,' grumbled Sir Henry. 'They're not going to knock at your door, you know.'

'Thank you, Sir Henry,' said Sergeant Flower, and added under his breath, 'for pointing out the blinking obvious. Good night.' He picked up his car keys with a sigh and then he remembered his cup of tea. It was a shame to let it go cold. Sir Henry's hordes of robbers, he decided, could have another five minutes' fun and games before he came looking for them.

'Time for Operation Pizza!' whispered Sid as she shook the boys awake. A few minutes later they emerged from the shop under piles of pizza boxes. 'Now remember, boys,' said Sid in a whisper like a thousand hissing snakes, 'we've got to be REALLY QUIET!'

Professional soldiers given a dangerous, top-secret mission would not have immediately chorused, 'Let's call Sid.' If there was a twig to snap or a leafy pile to rustle, Sid's foot would find it. Her hair was so orange it almost glowed in the dark and her round shape made flattening herself into the shadows almost impossible. But somehow the trio made it all the way to the Bullionburgers' gates without discovery or mishap.

'Now to test our plan,' said Sid as they set down their boxes. She tore a hunk from the first pizza, put her face to the bars and whistled softly. Oli and Skipjack waited nervously. Would the wolf come quietly? Would he even like pepperoni pizza?

The sound of claws on tarmac told them that the Bullionburger hound was on his way. He clattered to a halt by the gates and glared at them.

'Don't bark, dog,' Skipjack pleaded.

'Quick, give him some pizza,' urged Oli.

Sid tossed the piece she was holding through the bars.

The huge animal pricked up his ears, gulped the pizza down in one bite and turned back for more.

'See? He likes it,' said Sid with deep satisfaction. 'Everyone likes my pepperoni pizza. Now, off you go and find your tree, and I'll stay here and keep pooch happy. But hurry – we only brought six pizzas.'

As the boys sped away, Oli untied the knotted rope which he had wound around his waist. They had made a firm loop in one end of the rope, so when they reached the tree they were ready to throw the rope over the nearest branch, put the other end through the loop and pull it. Skipjack then climbed up, spurred on to almost superhuman speed by visions of the hound tiring of pizza and coming to look for some real meat. At the top of the wall he pulled the rope up and let the end fall on the inside so that he could use it to climb back out again. Then he jumped off the wall.

Meanwhile feeding time at the zoo was brought to an abrupt end by the engine hum of a slowly approaching car. Sid glanced about for a hiding place and saw that on either side of the gates grew a big bush, neatly clipped into a sphere. Sid scooped up the pizza boxes and jumped behind one of these green balls. The dog looked on, astonished: was the midnight feast over?

Seconds later a police car pulled up and Sergeant Flower climbed out, grumbling to himself. It was all very well for the mayor, tucked up in a nice, warm bed, to send him off to tackle dangerous criminals. Life wasn't fair. Full of bitter thoughts, Sergeant Flower approached the gates with the intention of having a quick peep through and then driving home to his own nice, warm bed.

The dog's eye view of recent developments on the other side of his gate was this: One minute a smiley lady had been feeding him delicious pizza. The next minute she had vanished and been replaced by a frowning man with no pizza. This alone was enough to dampen any dog's mood. And when that frowning man went so far as to grab the bars of the gate and peer through, the Bullionburger hound responded as any self-respecting guard dog would and threw itself at the gate in a frenzy of barking.

Sergeant Flower leapt away like a frightened frog and hopped back into his car. As he drove away he comforted himself with the thought that no one, but no one, would be able to put so much as one toe inside those walls without being minced alive.

Of course Skipjack had a lot more than one toe inside those walls.

'Did you hear that?' he squeaked. 'I'm going to be minced alive.'

'Sid must have run out of pizza,' whispered Oli. 'Can you see the Phantom Farter?'

'Not yet!' hissed Skipjack. 'I'll use the tracker and see if it farts.'

But instead of a welcome fart, all they heard was the dog, whose barks were growing louder and louder.

'Hurry up, Skip!'

'I'm hurrying!' Skipjack shoved the tracker into his pocket, grabbed the rope and shinned up, reaching the top of the wall just as the snarling super-canine reached the bottom.

'Phew!'

'The rope,' Oli reminded him.

Skipjack tried to pull up the rope but the dog snapped hold of the end with determined teeth. After a short tug-of-war, during which the boy nearly lost his balance and fell into the jaws of death, he was forced to give up.

They ran back towards the gates, but crashed into Sid hurrying the other way. Six pizza boxes went flying into the air.

'Any luck?' she asked, as they scrambled about picking everything up.

'Nope,' said Oli.

'Rats. It was such a smashing plan. Come on.'

So they legged it back

through the sleeping town, and had nearly reached the safety of Sid's shop when they turned a corner into a long street to find that they were not the only people up and about that night: the Gnome Guard patrol had just turned into the same street from the far end and was marching their way.

'About turn!' hissed Sid.

'Stop!' shouted Albert Grimble, and then, when that failed, 'They're running away! After them!'

'We'll take the next street,' panted Sid.

As it happened, this was the road where Reggie and the Grimbles lived.

Poor Reggie had spent the most boring night of his life sitting at his window watching the swag-bag gnome. As gnomes go, it was nice enough, but it did not provide enough action-packed drama to keep an audience interested for more than about thirty seconds. Reggie had been watching it for nearly five hours. He was bored, tired and hungry. In the kitchen, he

remembered, was half an onion pie left over from his supper. Reggie stood up, stretched and left his post.

Just then Sid and Oli charged past the Grimbles' house and Skipjack, who was bringing up the rear, glanced into their garden to enjoy its gnomelessness. There, to his surprise and dismay, he noticed a new gnome, standing by the pond with a swag-bag. Had the Gnome Freedom Army taught Mr Grimble nothing? How dare the man go straight out and buy a new gnome! After a quick glance behind, Skipjack was over the fence and in a trice the little chap was snuggled under his coat, being carried away to freedom. Only when Skipjack was sprinting to catch up with the others did he remember that Sid would not be very pleased about yet another rescue. He decided to keep the new gnome hidden until he could slip it into the tree house unnoticed.

Thirty seconds after Sid and the boys had whizzed by, and fifteen seconds after the Gnome Guard had thundered past in hot pursuit, Reggie returned to his post. He settled down into his chair, balanced the leftover onion pie on the windowsill and looked out.

The gnome was gone.

Reggie shot out of his seat and peered again. The gnome was still gone. It dawned on Reggie that all the peering in the world would not bring it back.

It has already been noted that Reggie was a particularly cool kind of cat-burglar, but even he was beginning to heat up. He started to pace the room, punching the palm of his left hand with the fist of his right. He told himself that Big Ben Baloney must have come along and pocketed the gnome. He would know for sure tomorrow, when Big Ben found the note and rang him. Until then he was *not* going to worry. He sat down again in his chair, started eating his onion pie, and worried.

Super-Gladys

After a delicious Sunday breakfast of triple-pepperoni pizza with extra cheese, Sid dropped the boys off at the rugby club, as arranged. They played a gruelling match against a club whose smallest player made Slugger Stubbins look like Tinker Bell the fairy, but they scraped a victory and limped off the field battered but happy.

Oli's mum had taken Tara and her mice to the *Total Talent* auditions early that morning and would not be back until the evening. As his older sister Becky's idea of Sunday lunch was a low-fat yogurt, Oli went home with Skipjack after rugby, for roast chicken followed by apple pancakes.

For Captain Grimble of the Gnome Guard, however, there was no time to enjoy fine food – duty called, more urgently than ever. He had come so close to catching the gnome-robbers last night, yet still they had slipped through his clutches. Then he had returned home to find that the gnome they had stolen had been from his very own garden! It was enough to drive a man potty. More determined than ever to win the war against the Gnome Freedom Army, Captain Grimble had drawn up a new patrol rota and was now busy dropping copies through the doors of his fellow Gnome Guarders.

This meant that he was not at home when Sergeant Flower telephoned. Reggie was there though, because Mrs Grimble had invited him over to share some onion pie.

'Hello?' whispered Mrs Grimble into the handset. There was a pause. 'Really? Oh, what good news, Sergeant. Thank you.'

She put the telephone down and turned to Reggie. 'Some of the gnomes have been found,' she squeaked. 'They're at the police station.'

Normally if Reggie Smith had the choice between (1) visiting a police station and (2) swimming a river full of crocodiles, he would go for the crocs. But normally police stations did not offer up diamonds the size of ping-pong balls.

Fighting down the urge to jump into the air and shout yippee, Reggie arranged his face into an expression of friendly pleasure. 'That's fantastic, Mrs G. Why don't I run you down there now? We can save your delicious pie till later.'

Mrs Grimble twiddled with her cardigan buttons, suddenly very pink. 'That would be lovely, Reggie,' she whispered at the floor. 'But do call me Gladys.'

And so it was that Mrs Gladys Grimble, who had hardly dared go near a sports car in her life for fear that it might bite her, found herself in the passenger seat of Reggie's beautiful red Morgan.

For the first five minutes she was completely speechless. Then she said, 'What a lovely car, Reggie. You must clean a lot of windows to afford this.'

Reggie chuckled. 'I do, Gladys, I do. I work my fingers to the bone.'

'Albert says it's not worth anyone doing an honest job these days when all you have to do to be rich is steal a few diamonds. He's very bitter about it.'

Reggie shook his head sadly. 'If only it was that

simple, Gladys. So, where did they find the gnomes?'

'In the park, yesterday afternoon. They've been checking them for clues and fingerprints.'

'Really? Did they find anything?' asked Reggie casually.

'Lots of fingerprints but they don't know whose, yet,' said Gladys.

They arrived at the police station to find Sergeant Flower standing on the counter struggling to keep control of the squabbling gnome-owners.

'Whose is this one?' he shouted above the din and he waved a red gnome in the air.

'It's mine!' shouted a voice.

'Liar! It's mine,' yelled another voice. 'My auntie gave it to me for Christmas.'

Sergeant Flower gave up. He held up a different gnome. 'What about this one?' he called.

'Oh,' squeaked Mrs Grimble, a little breathless. 'That's mine!'

Sure enough, the sergeant was holding up a grinning gnome with an eye-mask and a swag-bag. Reggie's spirits leapt.

'Here you are, Madam,' said Sergeant Flower, handing it down.

'Not so fast,' came a gruff voice from behind. A pair of huge knobbly hands reached down and gripped the tiny figure. 'That's my gnome.'

Mrs Grimble looked up, alarmed. Her fellow claimant loomed over her; a towering man with a big black beard, an eye patch and a scar down one cheek. He tightened his grip on the gnome. At first Gladys only held on because she was too shocked to move and when she realised that her rival was probably a pirate, her instinct was to let go at once and apologise.

Then her eye caught Reggie, who was staring from the gnome to the pirate with a look of

complete horror. Dear Reggie, her new friend
and fellow fan of onion pies, who had given her
this very gnome as a present. Poor Reggie, who
now looked so fearful that this precious token of
their friendship would be taken away for ever.

Gladys was filled with rage. How dare this ogre
try to rob her of Reggie's gnome? She clutched
the little statue with her thin white fingers and
glared at him. 'It's *my* gnome,' she told him. 'Let
go, you . . . nasty man!'

He glared back. 'I will not,' he growled and
gave the gnome a yank. But Gladys Grimble held
on with all her puny strength so that the yank
pulled her against the pirate, who lost his balance.
They both stumbled on to the floor
and the gnome went flying into
the air.

Reggie dived like a championship goalie but gravity was against him. The gnome smashed on to the floor. Reggie did not know whether to wait for the Black Star to come rolling out in full view of Sergeant Flower, grab it and try to run, or whether just to give up hope now and run.

But when he scanned the pottery debris there was no sign of the diamond. The gnome had been empty; it had not been Mrs Grimble's after all.

'Now, now,' said Sergeant Flower, looking disapprovingly at the mess of pirate, Gladys and gnome on the floor. 'Everyone keep calm.'

Reggie helped the furious Mrs Grimble to her feet. 'Never mind, Gladys,' he said, soothingly. 'Let's look at the other gnomes.' But there were no familiar figures at all in the identity parade on the sergeant's counter. Reggie frowned: where was the Black Star diamond gnome?

Mrs Grimble calmed down on the way home and even gave Reggie a little goodbye wave from her doorstep. Reggie managed to wave back, but with a smile as strained as a rubber band in a catapult. Then he went in through his own front door, closed it behind him, leant against it and cursed his bad luck. He needed a cup of tea. He stumped through the house to the kitchen at the back and stopped.

'Hello, Reg,' said Big Ben Baloney.

Reggie shot to the window and drew the curtains, before turning round and glaring.

'Are you crazy, coming here?' he demanded.

'Sorry, Reg, but I had nowhere else to go.' Ben shrugged. 'Knuckles McHefty from the Main Drain Gang is after me. I gotta lie low for a while.'

'How did you get in?'

'The usual way, Reg.'

Reggie now saw that his back door had been forced open.

'Thanks, Ben. And *why* haven't you been answering your phone?'

'Some geezer pinched it. You can't trust anyone these days.'

'Yeah, terrible, isn't it?' muttered Reggie. 'What I want to know is: have you got the gnome?'

'I was going to ask you the same question, Reg,' said Big Ben. 'I came last night, but it wasn't there. There's something about gnomes in this newspaper, though. I wondered if there was any connection.'

Reggie snatched Big Ben's newspaper and spread it out on the table.

BULLIONBURGER ROBBERY – NEW CLUE!

Police scientists are examining the Phantom Farter keyring (pictured below), which was left at the scene of Friday's crime. The keyring is currently being tested for fingerprints and enquiries are being made at Doctor Levity's joke shop. Also found was a coded list, which is being studied by expert code-breakers now in the hope that it may contain valuable information about the Gnome Freedom Army or the cat-burglar.

For the first time that day, Reggie Smith smiled. He recognised that keyring.

At about the same time that Reggie was discovering he had a visitor, Mr Grimble was delivering his last Gnome Guard rota. On his way home for tea, he passed a newsagent's and decided to pop in for a paper. The headline shouted out at him:

BULLIONBURGER ROBBERY – NEW CLUE!

For the first time that day, Albert Grimble smiled. He recognised that keyring.

Trouble in the Tree House

At about the same time that Reggie was discovering he had a visitor and Mr Grimble was delivering his last rota (in other words at about five o'clock that Sunday afternoon) Oli and Skipjack were sitting in the tree house, frowning at the leftover gnomes.

They had arranged with Sid to repeat yesterday's gnome-release plan after lunch, and had set out with backpacks full of gnomes and hearts full of hope that their troubles would shortly be over. But Sid had intercepted them at the park gates with the news that Tara's policeman, disguised as a gardener, was spying on the Wild Garden. So they had put the plan into reverse.

'And even if we found somewhere else to put them,' Oli pointed out, 'what with the police and the Gnome Guard and half the town on the look-out, it's getting too dangerous –'

'Shh!' hissed Skipjack. 'Was that a car?'

Oli picked his way through the crowd of little statues to the window and opened it wide to look out. Dusk was already closing in and a mist was rising. He listened. 'Nothing,' he reported. 'They're not after us yet, Skip.'

'I feel like a hunted animal,' sighed Skipjack. 'I might be on the run for the rest of my life.'

'Don't worry, Skip – I'll run with you. Hey – talking of running, what about this for a plan: I've got a leftover postcard from our holiday in Scotland. We could write on it: "We've run away to be free in the Highlands. Lots of love, the Gnomes." Then we could send it to the newspaper and they'll print it and everyone will give up searching.'

Skipjack nearly forgot he was a wanted man and chuckled, 'Great! Then we can sneak this lot into the park next weekend with a note saying that Scotland was too cold and they were homesick.'

'The only problem –' Oli frowned – 'is

keeping them here in the meantime. Mr Grimble could so easily say something to the police about us. I wish we had a safer hiding place.'

'Shh – what's that?' demanded Skipjack.

'That' was the creak of the rope ladder.

'Someone's coming!' cried Skipjack. 'Quick! Shut the trap door!'

But it was too late. A man's head popped up into the tree house.

'Hello, lads,' said Reggie Smith with a grin. 'Nice place you've got here.'

The boys were surprised and relieved. They had expected Mr Grimble, the police, the mayor, an armed Special Forces unit or the Prime Minister, but not the nice window cleaner with the cool car. 'Hi, Reggie,' they said as he climbed up through the hole.

Then Big Ben appeared, and went on and on appearing until the whole tree house seemed to be full of a human mountain. One of the things that made Reggie such a successful cat-burglar was that he didn't look like a criminal. Big Ben, on the other hand, looked like nothing else. As the boys gawped at all 6 foot 5 inches of solidness, they could not help wondering if they might be in Trouble after all.

Reggie looked round at all the gnomes and chuckled. 'Hey, lads! What a haul! This is Big Ben, by the way. He's a pal of mine.'

Big Ben grinned, showing several missing teeth, and gave the boys a little wave. On the

way to Pond Lane, Reggie had given him strict instructions not to say anything or do anything. 'They're nice lads, Ben, and I don't want you frightening them.'

Now Reggie smiled at the boys. 'You might be wondering why we're here,' he said.

The boys nodded, still unable to take their eyes off Big Ben.

'The fact is,' explained Reggie cheerfully, 'we saw the photo of the Phantom Farter in the newspaper and we put two and two together, you might say.'

'You mean they've found it?' Skipjack gasped.

'They have indeed. I can see you're getting a bit nervous, and rightly so. Who knows when the police might find your fingerprints or break that code? Hold on . . .' He cocked his head to one side as if listening intently. 'Is that a siren I can hear?'

Poor Skipjack went pale, but after a few seconds Reggie shook his head.

'False alarm. Where were we?'

'Nervous,' squeaked Skipjack.

Reggie nodded. 'That's right. Very nervous

indeed. So we thought we'd come and help.'

'Er, thanks,' ventured Oli. 'How?'

'I was just coming to that,' said Reggie. 'How about us getting rid of all these gnomes for you? My car's parked outside. We could just pop 'em all in a bag and take 'em back to my place. End of gnomes, end of worries!' He beamed.

'Would you really do that for us?' cried Skipjack.

'Of course we would. It wasn't so long ago that we were lads, eh Ben?'

Ben nodded.

'We used to get into all sorts of scrapes, eh Ben?'

Ben nodded again vigorously and rolled his eyes as if remembering a long run of youthful mischief. The boys exchanged raised eyebrows, both wondering if he was quite right in the head.

'That would be fantastic,' said Oli. 'And it would only be for a week, till all the fuss has died down. Then we'll come and take them to the park.'

'You must promise', said Skipjack, 'to be really careful with them. They've got to go back to their owners, because taking other people's things is always a no-no.'

'You can count on us, lads,' said Reggie, blushing slightly.

'Thanks, Reggie,' said Oli. 'We knew you were a friend from the moment you gave us a ride in your Morgan. I'll go down and get a bag.'

'No need, Oli. We've come prepared!' Reggie pulled a plastic sack out of his coat pocket and shook it open. 'In they go!' he said cheerfully, while scanning the room for the Black Star gnome.

The boys began passing the figures to Big Ben, who placed them one by one in Reggie's sack.

'Mind this one,' said Skipjack as he handed over the giant Bullionburger gnome. 'It's really heavy.'

Big Ben, forgetting his vow of silence, remarked in a friendly way, 'My, that's a big gnome.'

'The biggest in town,' chuckled Oli, picking up another with an eye-mask and a swag-bag. 'We took it from the Bullionburgers' house on Friday night.'

'Fancy that!' said Big Ben. 'The same night Reg was there, eh Reg?'

While all this was happening in the tree house, Mrs Gladys Grimble had remembered the onion pie that she and Reggie had left uneaten in their rush to the police station and she was taking it next door for him. Reggie's house was dark, but she thought he must be home because the back door stood ajar. Then she noticed that the lock had been forced.

A change had come over Gladys Grimble since her lunchtime grapple with the pirate. Now, instead of fluttering away squeaking with fear, she stepped boldly inside. Who dared to break into her lovely Reggie's house? Gladys set the pie down on the table and picked up a heavy frying pan. Thus armed, she set off to confront the wicked intruder.

She was disappointed not to find a burly villain lurking behind any of the doors but she perked up when she saw, in the bedroom, an enormous cupboard: the perfect hiding place. Frying pan raised in readiness, she threw the doors open and was amazed to find not a cowering criminal but shelf upon shelf of gnomes. All exactly the same: all kitted out with eye-masks and swag-bags, all grinning cheekily.

Gladys Grimble lowered her frying pan and frowned. Something was not right here. Then she noticed a cardboard box on the floor of the cupboard. She put her weapon down on the bed, pulled out the box and opened it.

Inside was a length of thin rope, several pairs of fine rubber gloves, a black balaclava and a large brown envelope. Gladys opened the envelope and shook out its contents. A sheaf of newspaper cuttings fluttered to the floor. As she knelt to read them, the headlines leapt from the pages:

CAT-BURGLAR STRIKES AGAIN!

DIAMONDS WORTH MILLIONS STOLEN!

ANOTHER SNATCH BY THE CAT!

One glance at the cuttings told the dreadful truth. Her lovely Reggie was a low-down jewel thief. Their special bond, forged from shared love of onion pie and gnomes, was fake.

Gladys rose, a volcano of boiling outrage. As she stormed back downstairs she could hear Reggie's voice inside her furious head, cooing, 'You're an angel, Mrs G.'

'Angel indeed. I'll give you angel, Reggie Smith,' muttered Gladys. Armed with her trusty frying pan, she hid behind the kitchen door, and waited.

While one half of the Grimbles was planning Grievous Bodily Harm on her next-door neighbour, the other half was marching across the Biggles lawn towards the tree house, planning the same thing on Oli and Skipjack.

In the tree house itself, the stunned silence that had followed Big Ben's bombshell was now broken by Skipjack.

'So Reggie's the *cat-burglar*!' he exclaimed.

On the grass below the window, Mr Grimble halted.

Reggie opened his blue eyes very wide. 'Who, me?' He chuckled, shaking his head. 'I wish I was, Skipjack my friend. I'd be sunning myself in the Bahamas now instead of cleaning windows.'

But Skipjack was on a roll. 'Why else would you have been at the Bullionburgers' house on Friday night?' he demanded. 'Anyway, we saw you go past. I'm sure it was you, wasn't it, Oli?'

'Of course it was,' said Oli bitterly. 'Reggie's the cat-burglar all right – that explains the Morgan. Fine friend you turned out to be, Reggie. So what have you done with all the diamonds?'

'Yeah, where's the Black Star, Reggie?' asked

Skipjack. 'Did you give it to Ben to sell for you? Is he your gate?'

'Fence, I'm a fence,' corrected Ben.

'Fence, then,' said Skipjack impatiently. 'Or have you stashed them somewhere?'

Mr Grimble was listening so hard his ears nearly burst. This could be the chance of a lifetime. If he was quick now, he might never have to drive another bus. He just had to hurry to wherever the diamonds were hidden and pinch them while Reggie was still busy with the boys.

Reggie thought fast. All that mattered was getting out of here with the right gnome. He considered offering the boys money in return for their silence but one glance at Oli's furious face told him they would not be bought.

But Oli, glaring at Reggie, suddenly guessed the truth. It's here! The Black Star is hidden in one of these gnomes – that's why Reggie came. But which one? His eyes swept quickly over the crowd of gnomes.

Reggie said airily, 'The diamonds? Oh, they're at my house, safe in bed.' But Oli noticed Big

Ben's eyes dart to the very gnome he was holding in his hand. Quick as a flash, he threw it out of the open window.

Down below, Mr Grimble was hurrying away to Reggie's house when he was hit on the head by a falling gnome and knocked out cold. The gnome, which was made of stronger stuff than the bus driver, rolled unbroken into a patch of long grass.

'Quick, get that gnome!' shouted

Reggie. He made a dive for the trap door and slid down the rope ladder without touching the rungs. Big Ben lumbered down after him and together they began searching for the precious statue.

'Bomb them!' yelled Oli. He picked up the nearest gnome and hurled it through the window at Big Ben, missing him by millimetres. Skipjack aimed another one which struck Reggie on the leg.

'What's that dark thing in the grass that they keep tripping over?' wondered Skipjack as he aimed the Bullionburger giant at Big Ben. 'Bullseye!' he shouted as gnome met head, but while the statue shattered into a thousand pieces, Ben carried on as if nothing had happened.

Then a shout came from Reggie: 'Got it!'

'Nice one, Reg!' called Big Ben.

'Thief!' yelled Oli.

Reggie glanced up at the tree-house window and grinned at the two angry faces glaring out at him. 'Ben, I think we need to keep our two young friends away from the phone until we've had time to escape. Do something about this ladder, will you?'

Oli dived for the rope ladder and started hauling it up frantically but Big Ben Baloney gripped the end as it rose.

'Let go, Oli!' warned Reggie, just in time. Ben gave the ladder such a mighty tug that the nails holding it in place at the top flew out and the ladder fell to the ground.

'Sorry, lads,' called Reggie. 'Ben? Catch.' He tossed the precious gnome to his partner. 'I'm going home to collect the rest of the loot.'

'OK, Reg. See you in Amsterdam.'

'You'll never get away with this!' shouted Oli, but the boys could only watch furiously as the two crooks split up and escaped into the dusk.

Suddenly Skipjack said, 'What *is* that thing down there?' He pointed to the dark shape in the grass which was now starting to move. There was something deeply creepy about the way it seemed to rise slowly out of the misty ground, like a monster from the bowels of the earth.

Finally the thing was standing upright, swaying slightly and rubbing its head, and the boys realised what it was.

'It's Mr Grimble!' exclaimed Oli in amazement. 'What's he doing here?'

'He can rescue us,' said Skipjack. 'Hey, Mr Grimble! Help!'

But Albert Grimble didn't even hear, because inside his head a much louder voice than Skipjack's was still shouting, 'Diamonds!'

'Diamonds!' repeated Mr Grimble. 'I must have the diamonds!' And like a man possessed, he staggered back to his car. He might still be in time.

'Thanks a lot!' Oli yelled after him. He turned to Skipjack. 'We've got to stop them all, Skip. We've got to get out of here.'

'Can we jump?' wondered Skipjack, craning his neck over the trap door.

'Not without a parachute,' said Oli.

'Can we climb down the tree?'

'Impossible, without being Reggie,' said Oli bitterly.

'In that case, there's only one thing for it. We must take our jeans off.'

Oli could not see how being stuck in a tree house with his jeans off would be any better than

being stuck in a tree house with his jeans on, and said so.

'I saw this film,' explained Skipjack, undoing his belt, 'about two guys who were locked in an upstairs room. And they escaped through the window by tying the ends of their trousers together and making a kind of rope.' He pulled off his jeans. 'Hurry up, Oli.'

While Oli de-trousered, Skipjack hunted about for the nails which had held the rope ladder in place.

'You look for something to hammer them in, Oli,' he said.

Oli cast his eye over

Tara's animal collection and spotted a big stone in a terrarium. Ignoring the glare of a lizard annoyed at having its furniture removed, he took out the stone and used it to bang two nails through the end of one trouser leg into the wooden edge of the trap door. Meanwhile Skipjack tied the second leg to one of the legs of the other pair with a scrap of string from his pocket. Sure enough, the resulting 'rope' was just long enough for the two boys to slip down and drop safely from the end.

'That was brilliant, Skip,' said Oli as he picked himself up.

'The old ones are always the best,' agreed Skipjack

'Now, let's go and phone the police, quick.'

But halfway to the house, Skipjack stopped and grabbed Oli's arm.

'If we tell the police about Reggie,' he said, 'We'll have to tell them we stole the gnomes.'

12

Last Gnome Lost

Oli's heart sank. 'But if we don't phone the police, Reggie and Ben will get away.'

'Does that matter?' asked Skipjack. 'The Bullionburgers can afford hundreds of new diamonds and so can Mrs Raisin of Kalamistan, or whatever she's called. I don't want to go to prison, Oli.'

'Me neither,' said Oli.

So the boys stood in their boxer shorts among the wreckage of gnomes strewn about on the grass, not knowing what to do.

Behind Reggie's back door, Gladys Grimble waited, armed with a heavy frying pan and feeling volcanic. She was just making a mental tally of all the onion pies she had baked for the undeserving Reggie when she heard footsteps.

Gripping her weapon even
tighter, she gritted her teeth
and waited for the door to
open. Then she stepped
forwards and struck. BONG!
Reggie went down like a ten-
pin. The delighted Gladys Grimble kissed her
frying pan and was about to return home to
telephone the police when she heard another set

of footsteps approaching
the kitchen door. An
accomplice! Resuming her
ambush position, Mrs
Grimble waited for the
moment to strike, then BONG! A second body
hit the deck. Were there any more? Mrs Grimble
listened. Yes! Yet another crook was jogging up
the path. This one paused, filling the whole
doorway. Mrs Grimble stood on
her tiptoes.

'Reg?' called a deep voice. 'I
forgot my car keys. They're
here on the table. I'll just –'
BONG! As the crash of this last

body meeting the floor died away, the sound of sirens filled the air. The police had arrived.

Mrs Grimble put down her weapon, switched on the lights and pattered through the house to open the front door. A quartet of constables loomed into view, led by the solid Sergeant Flower.

''Evenin', ma'am,' said he. 'We've had a report that the cat-burglar lives here, under the name of Reggie Smith.'

'Yes, that's right. I'm Mrs Grimble, from next door. I've just knocked him out. And his two accomplices.'

Sergeant Flower's eyebrows wobbled. 'Knocked 'em out, ma'am?'

'Yes. With a frying pan. They're in the kitchen.'

Then Sergeant Flower remembered that he had last seen this woman in his police station, doing battle with a black-bearded skyscraper. She clearly had a talent for this sort of thing. So he just said, 'Perhaps you could show us, ma'am.'

'Certainly, officer,' said Mrs Grimble. 'This way.'

The policemen followed her through the house to the kitchen, where she pointed to a pile of bodies in the back doorway.

'There they are,' she said proudly. 'Oh my goodness!' Her hand flew to her mouth.

'Is something the matter, ma'am?' enquired Sergeant Flower.

'That's my husband!' Gladys exclaimed.

Sergeant Flower peered at the heap and saw that in the middle of it, sandwiched between a slim, fair-haired man and a twenty-stone giant, was the bus driver. He shook his head. 'So it is. Fancy that: Mr Grimble – a cat-burglar.

Wonders will never, as they say, cease. All right, lads, drag the big one off those others – they'll be flat as pancakes under all that. And don't look now, but I think they're coming round.'

Sure enough there were signs of life from the bodies on the floor. Reggie's eyes were creaking open and Mr Grimble was mumbling, 'Diamonds. I must have the diamonds.' Sergeant Flower's eyes narrowed and he made a note in his little black book.

The constables stood ready with handcuffs as one by one Gladys's victims staggered to their feet, rubbing their heads and moaning. Their attacker, however, was remorseless.

'Reggie Smith! How dare you trick everyone into believing you were an honest window cleaner when you're nothing but a common thief!' she exclaimed. Reggie tried on his most irresistible smile but she was unmoved. 'Using my gnomes and my garden, too,' she cried. 'You should be ashamed of yourself!'

Then she turned on her husband. 'And you, Albert Grimble,' she continued, 'creeping about in the dark like that – whatever were you up to?'

'Er, I . . .' began Mr Grimble, slightly dazed by this new, commanding Gladys. He tried to think of a good excuse but his head ached terribly and his brain cells seemed to shrivel up under his wife's glare.

Meanwhile Oli and Skipjack, having confessed everything to Sergeant Flower down the telephone, had decided that if they were going to be arrested anyway they may as well enjoy the fun at Reggie's house before being locked up. So they pedalled there as fast as possible and arrived panting in the kitchen to find five policemen, one cat-burglar (in handcuffs), one fence (same), one bus driver (same again) and one Mrs Grimble.

'Oh good,' puffed Oli. 'You weren't too late to catch them.'

'And you've arrested Mr Grimble too,' said Skipjack, pleased. 'Quite right. He only came here to steal Reggie's diamonds.'

'Albert!' cried Mrs Grimble.

'That's a lie!' shouted her husband.

Sergeant Flower consulted his notebook. '"Diamonds, I must have the diamonds",' he quoted.

Oli and Skipjack nodded eagerly. 'That's just what he was saying at the tree house,' said Oli.

Reggie tutted. 'Really, Mr G. And I thought you were a fine upstanding citizen.'

'I am a fine upstanding citizen,' protested Albert Grimble, but nobody wanted to believe him, not even his wife.

The sergeant turned to Reggie. 'Why don't you be a fine upstanding citizen too and tell us what you've done with the Black Star?'

'I'd love to help, Sarge, honest I would,' said Reggie. 'But I don't know what you're talking about.'

'Yes, he does!' cried Oli. 'And we know where it is: Big Ben's got it, in a gnome. He was going to take it to Amsterdam.'

'Aha. Was he now? Search him, someone.'

The swag-bag gnome was quickly found in Big Ben's overcoat pocket and, to Skipjack's distress, smashed by a heavy boot. Everyone held their breath, expecting to see a diamond the size of a ping-pong ball.

The gnome was empty.

After a moment's puzzled silence, Oli said,

'I don't understand. There must have been two identical gnomes in the tree house, and they took the wrong one.' He frowned at the broken pieces on the floor and then he noticed something – a small piece of paper half hidden among the crumbs of pottery.

'Look!' he cried, pointing. Sergeant Flower picked up the slip and examined it.

'Aha, another coded message. We'll soon have this cracked.' He sealed the note in a small plastic bag, pocketed it and turned to one of his men. 'Take yourself off to Number 18 Pond Lane and search in and around the tree house for another gnome like this one. Now then,' he continued, turning back to Reggie, 'what about the Bullionburger diamonds?'

'Come on, Sarge,' said Reggie with a charming smile, 'if I'm the crook, as you suspect, then you and I are on opposite sides of this game. I'm not supposed to help you win it.'

'We can help!' cried Skipjack. 'In the tree house he said they were here, safe in bed.'

'Aha!' Leaving one of his men on guard in the kitchen, the sergeant led a stampede up the narrow stairs. Soon the bedroom air was thick with flying feathers and mattress stuffing.

'It's like a giant pillow fight,' giggled Skipjack as the boys watched from the door.

'They won't find anything though,' said Oli thoughtfully. 'Reggie wouldn't make it that easy.'

Sure enough, turning Reggie's bedroom into a blizzard of plumage revealed nothing sparkly at all. Hot and frustrated, the boys in blue trooped back down to the kitchen, followed by Oli and Skipjack.

'All right, turn out his pockets,' ordered Sergeant Flower.

Unlike the pockets of someone else we could mention, Reggie's contained only three items: a wallet, a mobile phone and a set of keys.

'Aha,' said Sergeant Flower, picking up the first two. 'These should provide some clues.'

But Oli and Skipjack were staring at the set of keys, or rather, at the keyring which held them.

It was a Phantom Farter.

'Look,' said Skipjack. 'The little tracker's missing.'

Oli's mind went back to the potato-trench day, when Reggie had first seen Skipjack's Phantom

Farter. A voice echoed in his head: 'It would come in handy if you ever buried treasure and had to find it again.'

Suddenly, Oli knew where the diamonds would be. 'They're in the other kind of bed,' he cried. 'The *flower* bed!' He grabbed the keyring, ran outside and began pacing along Reggie's overgrown back garden, pressing the keyring repeatedly.

Sergeant Flower and his men, Mr and Mrs Grimble, Reggie, Ben and of course Skipjack all

crowded out of the door to watch.

Halfway down the garden, muffled farts came from below.

Oli looked up with a grin. 'Found them!' he said.

'Aha,' announced Sergeant Flower. 'Right, find a spade!'

A spade was found and after a brief digging operation yet another swag-bag gnome was unearthed, and then another and another.

'*Three* gnomes full,' Oli whispered to Skipjack. 'For once that blogging Nevis was telling the truth: he really *did* have loads of diamonds in his safe.'

'No, he was telling the truth about his rocket-fuelled bottom as well, remember?' Skipjack whispered back, and then winced as Sergeant Flower bashed all three gnomes on the head with the back of his spade.

'I wish he wouldn't keep doing that,' he sighed.

In the debris of each gnome lay a black velvet drawstring bag. Sergeant Flower picked up the first one, untied it and felt about inside. He pulled out the farting tracker, chuckled and pocketed it. Then he shook the contents of the bag gently on to the palm of his hand.

They sparkled in the moonlight like a sky full of stars.

'Diamonds!' breathed the boys.

Sergeant Flower chuckled again and poured the gems back into the bag, which he tied securely and popped into the chest pocket of his uniform. He looked pleased. For just a while, the spotlight of success would be shining on him and not on that pompous old windbag Sir Henry Widebottom, the mayor.

He ruffled Oli's hair. 'Nice work, sonny. All right, lads, take them down to the station.'

'This is an outrage!' shouted Mr Grimble as he was led away. 'I haven't stolen anything! What about these two boys? Why aren't you arresting them for stealing my gnomes?'

Sergeant Flower hesitated. He was a fair man and, much as he objected to being told his business by a bearded bully like Albert Grimble, he had to admit the man had a point.

But before he could respond, Reggie broke in. 'Firstly, Mr G., you don't need to steal something to get yourself arrested. They can do you for trespass with the *intention* to rob. Trust me – I'm an expert. Secondly, Sarge, I happen to know that the boys only borrowed those gnomes because they were trying to find the diamonds. They were on to me from the start, you see.'

'Is that a fact?' nodded Sergeant Flower, eyeing the boys with a twinkle.

'It is. So go easy on 'em, eh?' And with a farewell shrug at Oli, he was gone, followed by the glaring Albert Grimble.

Gladys had watched all the action with great enjoyment, especially the part where her husband was bundled off to the police station. Now she turned to the sergeant.

'Thank you, officer. I'll just take my pie, and then I'll be off next door.'

'It smells delicious,' remarked Sergeant Flower as he handed it to her. 'Has it got onions in it?'

'Yes,' said Mrs Grimble. 'Lots.' She paused and cocked her head. 'Do you like onion pie, officer?'

'It's my favourite thing,' the sergeant told her.

She smiled. 'Then I'll make you one and bring it to the station. Goodbye.'

She had just left when Sergeant Flower's

mobile rang. He had a brief conversation with the caller, during which he said only 'Aha' in a variety of tones. This was maddening for the two listening boys and Skipjack might have snatched the phone to hear the news for himself if Sergeant Flower hadn't rung off.

'Well,' he told them, 'the Black Star wasn't in any of the gnomes you stole – sorry – "*borrowed*". We'll just have to keep looking.' He glanced at his watch. 'Come on. You two need to get home. Mind you explain all this to your parents – I'll be paying them a call in the morning.'

'Will we go to prison?' asked Skipjack in a small voice.

Sergeant Flower scratched his head. 'You boys have been stealing,' he replied. 'And stealing is against the law.'

Their faces fell.

'On the other hand,' continued Sergeant Flower, 'you owned up, which was brave of you, and you helped me find the Bullionburger diamonds *and* catch the world's best cat-burglar. So on balance . . .'

'Yes?'

'I've decided not to send you to prison.'

'Phew!'

'But I do want you to pay for all those smashed-up gnomes. OK?'

'OK, Sergeant Flower. Thank you.'

'My pleasure,' chuckled the sergeant. 'Now, off you go home, before you get into any more trouble.' And he waved them off on their bikes.

'I never thought I'd be so happy to be giving away all my savings to a bunch of gnome-owners,' announced Oli as they rode away, but as he cycled further his relief gave way to puzzlement. What *had* happened to the gnome with the Black Star diamond in it? If it wasn't among the ones already at the police station, and Reggie didn't have it, and it wasn't one of the leftovers at the tree house, where was the last gnome?

Then, just as they were nearing his house, the lights flashed on in Oli's brain. Instead of slowing down to turn into his driveway, he speeded up, whizzing straight past his gate.

'Why aren't you stopping?' asked Skipjack.

'Because I'm coming to your house,' replied
Oli. 'To look for a gnome.'

'Gnome?' squeaked Skipjack. 'What gnome?'

'It's no good pretending you haven't got it,
'cos I know you have,' panted Oli, pedalling
hard. 'I've worked it out and it's the only
possible answer. You always liked that swag-bag
gnome the best.'

They arrived neck and neck at Skipjack's
house, burst through the front door together and
raced up the stairs to his bedroom. Oli knew
where his friend hid secret stuff, and in a trice he
was standing on Skipjack's chair and feeling
about on top of his cupboard.

'Got it!' he exclaimed and held up the missing
gnome.

'Don't drop him!' cried Skipjack.

'I won't. Why didn't you tell Sergeant Flower
you had it?'

'I didn't want him to be smashed like the
others,' said Skipjack sadly.

Oli shook the gnome. There was a muffled
knocking sound.

'It's in there,' he said.

'I know it is. I don't care.'

'Think of the reward. You could buy a hundred gnomes.'

'I don't want a hundred gnomes. I want this gnome. He's got a special smile.'

Oli turned the gnome upside down. 'What if we could get the diamond out without breaking him? Look, there's a round patch underneath where Reggie sealed it. If we could scrape that away we could make a hole. Then you could have the reward *and* the gnome. OK?'

After a long pause Skipjack agreed. 'You try, Oli. I'd be too nervous.' So Oli took out his penknife and started working on the gnome. The clay which had been used to seal it up crumbled quite easily and soon it had all been chipped away. Oli turned the gnome the right way up and shook it gently.

On to the floor fell a black velvet bag. Skipjack picked it up and fumbled with the strings. Then he reached into the bag and pulled out an enormous diamond. The boys gasped. Skipjack held the diamond up to the light. It glittered brilliantly in a thousand dazzling colours.

'The Black Star,' whispered Skipjack.

'It really is the size of a ping-pong ball,' breathed Oli. 'No wonder it's priceless.'

They exchanged glances.

'I wonder if it's easy,' said Skipjack with a gleam in his eye, 'to get a fence.'

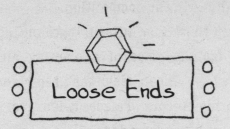

Loose Ends

Note on Tara's pillow that night:

Hi T,

Here is your silence money, plus extra for getting rid of that policeman in the park.

You were awesome.

Oli.

PS: Sorry you didn't win Total Talent. I bet the Queen would have liked your mice the best.

Letter to Tara on Buckingham Palace paper, received three days later:

Dear Miss Biggles,

Her Majesty the Queen has asked me to thank you for your kind letter and to tell you how much she enjoyed watching your mice on television. She agrees that they are *very* talented and she is sorry that they did not win the competition.

Regarding your offer to sell Togo and Pogo to Her Majesty for the price of a one-way air ticket to Timbuktu, the Queen feels that they would not be happy at Buckingham Palace: it isn't very cosy and there are far too many dogs.

She wishes you all the very best in your future adventures,

Yours sincerely,

Sylvia Salver

Personal Secretary to Her Majesty the Queen

Letter to Skipjack on police station paper, received two weeks later:

Dear Skipjack,

I believe this keyring and this list belong to you. If you ever want a job in our Secret Codes Department, they'd be delighted to have you.

Thanks to you and Oli for paying up so quickly for the broken gnomes. Mrs Grimble, by the way, says you can keep the swag-bag gnome – she never wants to see it again for as long as she lives.

I also enclose a nice big cheque for you and Oli to share — your reward from the Sultana of Kalamistan for finding the Black Star.

Best wishes

Inspector Flower

Letter to Oli on HM Prison Wormwood Scrubs paper, sent with a small package two months later:

Dear Oli,

I know you're really angry with me and I'm sorry. I just thought you'd like to know that thanks to you and Skipjack I'm giving up on crime and going straight. The Gnome Freedom Army was too much for me.

Big Ben's in here with me — we're helping out in the prison garden. I'm learning to plant flowers instead of diamonds (ha-ha). When we get out we're going to set up a gardening business together.

I sold the Morgan, of course, but here's something I made for you in the prison modelling club so

that your memories of me aren't all bad.
Take care Oli, and keep that Skipjack under
control.
Yours,
Reggie.

Oli opened the little parcel. Inside was a bright
red miniature Morgan. He smiled.

MORE TALES OF TROUBLE

MUM TROUBLE!

Oli wants to swap his mum for someone who'll let him eat loads of pepperoni pizza and watch *Real Blood Bath Murders* on telly.

Mother 44 drives a tank and trains secret agents. But she's also hatching an evil anti-children plot – and she's looking for a boy to help.

When the Mum Shop's Matcher puts them together, it's trouble!

SPOOKY TROUBLE!

Lord and Lady Spiffing want lots of ghosts − to thrill
the tourists.

Oli wants just one ghost − to win a bet with his sister.

Skipjack doesn't want any ghosts − but thanks to the
Spookoscope, he's got one.

If the ghosts aren't sorted by sundown,
there'll be trouble!